F
ROO

Roosevelt, Elliott,
1910-

Murder in the west
wing.

$18.95

MURDER
in the
WEST
WING

MURDER
in the
WEST
WING

An Eleanor Roosevelt Mystery

Elliott Roosevelt

St. Martin's Press • New York

Library of Congress Cataloging-in-Publication Data

Roosevelt, Elliott
        Murder in the west wing : an Eleanor Roosevelt mystery / Elliott
    Roosevelt.
                p.   cm.
        "A Thomas Dunne book."
        ISBN 0-312-08144-8 (hardcover)
        1. Roosevelt, Eleanor, 1884–1962—Fiction.   I. Title.
    PS3535.O549M87   1992
    813'.54—dc20   92-26155
                                                                    CIP

First Edition: December 1992

10 9 8 7 6 5 4 3 2 1

MURDER
in the
WEST
WING

I

In the later years of her life, when Mrs. Roosevelt looked back over her White House years, she had some difficulty deciding which was the best year, which was the worst.

The bad years were easy enough to identify. They were of course the war years, the years when she shared the anxiety that every mother suffered, when her sons' lives were at risk almost every day, in combat; the years also when she watched her husband's health deteriorate under the crushing weight of his responsibilities, and she could find no way to ease his burden. Mrs. Roosevelt did not look back with joy on those years.

She liked to think about the good years, and it was difficult to choose one from another.

Coming to the White House in 1933, she had faced her new position with trepidation.

She was no longer the shy, gawky woman she had been during the first two decades of her marriage. She had developed grace under pressure, but more important, she had

1

acquired sure personal and political instincts. More important yet, she had adopted a political and social agenda. She knew what she wanted to achieve.

Trepidation remained, just the same. She knew she was no great beauty in the style, say, of Lou Hoover, or Grace Coolidge, or Edith Wilson. Louis Howe insisted she *was* a beauty to anyone who came close enough to her to really know her, but that didn't help much, because few people were able to get that close.

She entered the White House with uncomfortable misgivings, and many months would pass before she began to feel even a little confident.

What was more, she was uncertain as to whether or not Franklin could govern effectively in the crisis of 1933.

Many thoughtful people said her husband was President by accident, elected for no other reason but that the people had turned away from President Hoover in blind frustration and would return to sound Republicanism in 1936. As astute a pundit as Walter Lippmann wrote that Franklin D. Roosevelt had no powerful mind but was only an amiable, well-meaning man whose chief qualification for the presidency was that he wanted it. The great Oliver Wendell Holmes had pronounced Franklin Roosevelt a "second-class intellect but a first-class temperament." It was impossible, too, to overlook the fact that he could not stand without steel braces strapped to his legs and even then needed someone beside him to catch him if he tottered. He was, really, confined to a wheelchair.

Triumphant though 1933 was—the inauguration, the Hundred Days, the beginning of recovery from the Great Depression—that year was not Mrs. Roosevelt's favorite.

Even at the end of the year, she was not positive that she and her husband had performed well.

Through 1934 and 1935 the First Lady grew more comfortable in her peculiar position.

There was reason for optimism about national and international affairs. In February 1934, the President created the Export-Import Bank to encourage international trade, particularly the export of U.S. agricultural products. In May 1935, the Congress enacted the President's proposal to create a Works Progress Administration—the WPA—which would give useful work to 8.5 million unemployed Americans. In July the President signed the National Labor Relations Act, which gave American workers the right to join labor unions and defined unfair employment practices. In August he signed the Social Security Act, as well as the Neutrality Act, which prohibited the sale of American arms and munitions to belligerents.

In 1934, Germany and Poland signed a ten-year nonaggression pact. Shortly the Soviet Union signed a similar pact with Poland and the Baltic States—and not long after joined the League of Nations. In 1935 Great Britain and Germany signed a naval treaty by which Germany agreed its navy would not exceed 35 percent of the strength of the British navy.

On the other hand—

That same year, 1934, was the year of the great Dust Bowl. Hundreds of millions of tons of topsoil were blown off the dry farmlands of the American Midwest, turning the sky red as far east as Washington. It was also the year in which German President Paul von Hindenburg died—and Chancellor Adolf Hitler was elected Führer. It was the year of Mao Tse-tung's Long March, which was perhaps significant but which few in the United States heard about. Japan renounced the Washington Naval Treaty of 1922 and declared itself at liberty to build as many warships as it wanted.

In 1935 the last of the Soviet show trials resulted in death sentences for the few old Bolsheviks who might have successfully opposed Stalin. From then on, his rule was absolute. Hitler renounced the disarmament terms of the Versailles Treaty and announced that Germany would immediately begin to build an army of thirty-six divisions. In October, Italy invaded Ethiopia. The League of Nations proved ineffective in halting the aggression.

An English Cassandra named Winston Churchill persisted in uttering shrill warnings about a coming war. It seemed a very remote possibility.

Also—

In these same years the first comic book was published, *Famous Funnies*, ten cents a copy. Robert Graves published *I, Claudius*. Tourists returning from France began smuggling in copies of Henry Miller's *Tropic of Cancer*—which customs agents would seize and confiscate if they found them. George Gershwin's *Porgy and Bess* opened on Broadway. The President turned on the lights for the first night baseball game at Crosley Field in Cincinnati—and the Reds won over the Phillies, 2–1. Charles Darrow began to sell a board game he had invented, called Monopoly. The first parking meter was installed, in Oklahoma City.

The year 1936 opened on a distressing note. Dear old King George V—"Grandfather England"—died. Even the Anglophobes of Boston and Chicago regretted the death of the innocuous old anachronism. On a more optimistic note, he was succeeded by the handsome, debonair Edward Albert

Christian George Andrew Patrick David, King Edward VIII, the world's most eligible bachelor. There was already an impediment to his success as king, but that was not yet public knowledge.

Mrs. Roosevelt entered the year 1936 with enthusiasm, confidence born of experience, and optimism that her husband would be reelected in November. In January of 1941, when their time in Washington was over, neither of them would yet be sixty years old, and they would retire to write their memoirs. She knew the President was planning to do that. She supposed she would, too.

If, later, she decided that 1936 was not her best year in the White House, it was a candidate for that honor, anyway.

Wednesday, March 4, 1936, began as an ordinary day. Even in the White House, with all its challenges and recurring crises, life settled into a routine.

The President's day usually began when he was wakened by Arthur Prettyman, his valet, who brought him the morning newspapers. Arthur helped him out of bed and into the bathroom, where the President shaved—having bathed the night before. Then, propped up by pillows, he received his breakfast tray and began his morning reading: first the newspapers if there was nothing urgent in his correspondence, then the morning's memos and letters.

The President always ate a hearty breakfast: ham and eggs, toast, juice, and coffee. Arthur would have brought in Fala by the time the President began to eat, and the President would toss scraps of bread and bacon to the Scottie, who would scamper around the room in delight. Missy Le-Hand, the President's private secretary and confidante, usually came in during breakfast and had a cup of coffee.

Missy lived on the floor above, in a modest suite, and often came down still wearing her nightgown and a peignoir. Most mornings, Mrs. Roosevelt also came in to see the President while he was eating breakfast and before he dressed. Usually she had an agenda: things to bring to his attention, requests for action. She came with a notepad, and as she talked she ticked things off and made notes.

After the President had eaten his breakfast and smoked his first Camel of the day, Arthur would help him dress and seat himself in his wood-and-steel wheelchair. Then, with powerful strokes of his muscular arms, the President would wheel himself briskly to the elevator. As buzzers sounded warning through the White House, the President of the United States would roll toward the Executive Wing and the Oval Office.

Although he loved to travel—so long a distance as to Texas or California, so short a distance as to the Mayflower Hotel to deliver a speech—the President's physical handicap made travel burdensome for him. More than most presidents, he kept to the Oval Office and at his desk.

Mrs. Roosevelt moved. She did the traveling that was hard for the President. She developed a reputation for it, for being the peripatetic First Lady.

On this March day in 1936, the President settled down in his office, facing a heavy schedule of visitors. Not one would come to offer anything. Every last one would come to the President to ask for something. Each man or woman would be received as if he or she were the first visitor of the day and the one whose problem was first in the President's mind.

The First Lady's day began with a breakfast at 8:30 for a delegation of farm-state congressmen's wives. They asked

her to make the President more vividly aware of the problems generated by the Dust Bowl. At 9:30 she was to leave the White House for the Smithsonian, where at 10:00 she would officially open an exhibition of Navajo weaving. Allowing fifteen minutes to view the weaving and express her admiration for it, she would leave the Smithsonian at 10:15. At 10:45 she would arrive at Bethesda Hospital for an all-too-short visit with the dying Louis McHenry Howe, friend, confidant, and adviser to both the Roosevelts for more than twenty years. From the hospital she would be driven to the Army-Navy Club, where she would attend a luncheon being given by the wives of high-ranking officers. She had no speech to make but would be expected to listen to arguments for increased army and navy expenditures.

Back at the White House before 2:00, she would try to give an hour to answering correspondence and dictating her newspaper column, "My Day." At 3:00 she would receive a delegation of Jewish women from New York who wanted her to be more aware of the injustices being perpetrated against German Jews under the Nuremberg Laws. She had a short speech to give them, prepared for her by the State Department and saying what she did not personally believe: that the government of the United States could do little to help the German Jews. At 3:45 she was to award a certificate of appreciation to a woman who was retiring as a maid on the White House staff after more than forty years of service—from the presidency of Benjamin Harrison to that of Franklin D. Roosevelt. At 4:00 she was scheduled to sit down before a microphone in a sound studio in the basement and make a record that would eventually be broadcast over various radio stations, appealing to Americans to give generously to the Community Chest. Cutting phonograph records was invariably a time-consuming, irritating procedure and always took more time than was scheduled for it. At 5:00 she was receiving the wife of the new Czechoslovak ambassador for tea.

She would have an hour to bathe and dress—to rest and gather her thoughts—before she left the White House at 7:30. She was the guest of honor, and of course featured speaker, at the annual dinner of the Washington-Baltimore-Richmond Area Conference of the American Association of University Women.

"We," she told the women of the association, "are fortunate indeed. While I have not the advantage of the college or university education all of you share, I was privileged to be educated in an English school and to be introduced by its headmistress, during travels on the Continent, to a world far larger than I had imagined existed. I learned that the world I knew as a girl was not universal—as you learned the same at your colleges and universities. I was shown the diversity of the world, as were you. I learned, to my surprise, that whatever we did and thought on Thirty-seventh Street in New York was not *necessarily* the right way of doing and thinking. Nor was the Boston way. Nor the Baltimore way. I suppose what we learn through education is perspective and tolerance. Maybe those are the most important things we learn. And allow me to suggest to you, ladies, that the tolerance we learned through education must never be forgotten but must be applied to our judgments, as we go about our daily lives, seeing and appraising and trying to reach intelligent and fair conclusions."

As the limousine returning the First Lady to the White House passed through the gate and approached the South

Portico, she glanced up and saw the light still burning in her husband's bedroom. It was 10:45, and if he was still awake, likely Missy was with him. He loved to listen to music, on the radio or on records, and Missy would stay with him to tune the radio or change the records, which he could not do except by laboriously lifting himself from the bed.

A White House policeman greeted her at the security desk at the south entrance. "Ma'am," he said, "Mr. Szczygiel has left word that he would like a word with you as soon as you return."

Stanislaus Szczygiel—it was pronounced "Siegal"—was an officer of the Secret Service. Of the men who protected the White House and First Family, he was not Mrs. Roosevelt's favorite. She detected in him a fondness for gin that she suspected Prohibition had not dimmed or impeded. Still, he had been with the Secret Service since the presidency of Theodore Roosevelt and was reputed to be a shrewd and effective man.

"Where is Mr. Szczygiel now?" she asked.

"In the kitchen, I believe, Ma'am," said the policeman.

"I shall see him there."

In the kitchen. Yes. With a key to the liquor cabinet and drinking from the White House supply, she dared say; and eating a sandwich from the White House larder, too, she would wager. She had learned shortly after this administration took over the White House that a very great number of people had been accustomed to eat and drink on the limited budget the Congress appropriated for official entertainment. By presidential order, the press corps no longer had unlimited access to food and drink, but the Secret Service continued to regard the kitchen as its own.

As she had expected, Stanislaus Szczygiel was sitting at

the big food-preparation table in the kitchen, eating a massive ham sandwich and drinking gin.

"Ah, Mr. Szczygiel," she said. "I understand you wish to see me."

"I do indeed, Ma'am," said Szczygiel. He rose and used a napkin to wipe his mouth before he spoke further. She thought of him as a square man: his ruddy pockmarked face square, his solid body square. He had a prominent nose, somewhat hooked. His close-cropped hair was graying blond. He was typical of the ethnic origin his name suggested, a Slovak, Slovene, Croat, Pole, or Serb, a representative of the best this origin offered: strong, stolid, honest, direct.

"Well, then?"

Szczygiel gestured toward the table, also toward the unlocked liquor cabinet, where an array of bottles could be seen. "Can I offer you something?" he asked.

Like most of the career people who worked all their lives in the White House, he apparently thought of the Roosevelts as guests and saw nothing ironical in his offering the First Lady a drink from what was, really, her own liquor cabinet.

"No, thank you, Mr. Szczygiel."

"A seat anyway," he said, pulling out a chair.

Mrs. Roosevelt was wearing a floor-length satin dress, pale green in color, with a string of pearls. She sat down at the kitchen table where the chefs prepared food.

Szczygiel took a sip of gin. "We have a serious problem with two members of the White House staff," he said.

"Oh?"

"Yes. One is dead, and the other has been arrested and charged with murder. The one who has been arrested asked that you come to D.C. police headquarters as soon as you can. That of course means tomorrow morning, but—"

"Who is it, for heaven's sake?"

"Thérèse Rolland. She is accused of murdering Paul Duroc."

It was past midnight when Mrs. Roosevelt and Agent Szczygiel arrived at District police headquarters. Szczygiel had telephoned ahead so the First Lady could hurry in through a side door and not be seen by the police reporters who lounged in the lobby of the building. An appearance by Mrs. Franklin D. Roosevelt at D.C. police headquarters after midnight would have been front-page news all over the country.

She was led through back corridors of the building to the office of Detective Lieutenant Edward Kennelly. Mrs. Roosevelt and Kennelly knew each other. They had worked together on the problem of the murder of Congressman Winstead Colmer, who had been murdered in the Oval Office in 1934.

Kennelly was a tall, florid Irishman with hair that had turned white when he was in his early forties. When the First Lady arrived, he was sitting behind his desk smoking a Lucky and drinking coffee from a grotesquely oversized mug.

"An honor it is again, as it is always," he said as he rose and extended his hand to Mrs. Roosevelt.

"Lieutenant Kennelly," she said, "my feelings about meeting you are much like those I feel when I see a doctor. I am pleased to see you, yet regret the occasion that brings us together."

Kennelly frowned. "Yes, a sad situation again. A young

man dead. A young woman locked in a cell back there." He shook his head. "It is too bad we don't meet on happier occasions. Can I offer you a cup of coffee?"

Mrs. Roosevelt smiled and nodded.

"Szczygiel?"

"I'll have a cup," said the agent. "Black as night, as I remember it."

Kennelly was grinning as he left the office to get the two cups of coffee.

The office was familiar to Mrs. Roosevelt. It was shabby: dusty, littered, the air heavy with the stench of cigarette smoke and the fetor of overflowing ashtrays. She wondered if the dead flies lying on the windowsill were the same ones she had noticed there in 1934.

She had required ten minutes to go to her room in the White House and change into a gray tweed suit and cream-colored blouse. On the way to headquarters in the car, Szczygiel had told her most of what he knew of the case: that Paul Duroc had collapsed in the men's room on the second floor of the West Wing. A heart attack had at first been suspected, but he was foaming at the mouth, and the doctor who examined him had detected the odor of cyanide poisoning. Duroc had died twenty minutes after he collapsed, without regaining consciousness. Lieutenant Kennelly had arrived about the time Duroc died. He had asked a few questions and had immediately placed Thérèse Rolland under arrest. Szczygiel had suggested in the car that Kennelly himself should explain why, rather than that Mrs. Roosevelt should hear the explanation secondhand.

Kennelly returned to his office, bearing steaming mugs of coffee.

"Well," said Mrs. Roosevelt, "I should like to know why

Miss Rolland is the suspect. She doesn't impress me as the sort of young woman who would commit murder."

Kennelly smiled gently. "Just what sort of young woman is the type who would commit murder?" he asked.

The First Lady returned his smile. "I assume you suspect her on the basis of some evidence, do you not?"

Kennelly nodded. He lit a cigarette. "Paul Duroc died of cyanide poisoning. The autopsy has already confirmed that. When a person swallows a dose of potassium cyanide, collapse comes within a minute or so. Never much longer. That means that Duroc swallowed the cyanide only a minute or so before he collapsed in the men's room. Probably he was feeling nauseous and rushed to the bathroom thinking he was going to vomit."

"And how does that suggest that Miss Rolland gave him the poison?"

"She had been with him in his office, with the door closed, for some time. I don't yet know how long, exactly. That wasn't unusual. It seems that he and she had formed a little habit of having a couple of drinks in his office before they left for the day. Always alone. When he hurried out of his office and across the hall to the men's room, she hurried to the ladies' room. She wasn't sick, though. She was carrying the glasses from which they had been drinking. She rinsed them out. Thoroughly. Not a trace of cyanide was found in either glass."

"That doesn't prove she killed him," said Mrs. Roosevelt.

"We looked for the container in which the cyanide had been brought to the office," Kennelly went on. "And we found it, in his wastebasket. There were no fingerprints on it. It is a small glass vial, like a pill bottle."

"In what sort of drink was the poison dissolved?"

"Bourbon," said Kennelly. "But let me explain. Potassium cyanide is a powder. Only a little bit of it is needed to cause death. A pinch of it, you might say. But it has to be dissolved in water and allowed to stand for five minutes to be effective. The police chemist explained this to me this evening. There has to be a chemical reaction between the powder and the water, changing potassium cyanide to hydrogen cyanide. Once the powder is dissolved, the water has to be drunk within an hour. But it has to stand in the water for five minutes before it is taken. She couldn't just put the powder in his drink. She had to put it in the water in the vial, and then pour the mixture in the drink."

"Doesn't the stuff taste awful?" Szczygiel asked.

"The bourbon would disguise the taste, partly anyway. Besides, one swallow would do it. Even if the bourbon tasted bad, his first swallow of it would carry enough cyanide to kill him. Particularly if it was a strong mixture."

"There is no direct evidence that Miss Rolland put the poison in Mr. Duroc's drink," said Mrs. Roosevelt.

"Who else could have done it?" asked Kennelly. "Only the two of them were in his office."

"Maybe he committed suicide."

"If he did that, why did he either handle the glass vial with gloves or wipe off the fingerprints?"

"The case is not convincing, Lieutenant Kennelly."

"All right. Let me add another element to it. Duroc has swallowed cyanide poison. He is nauseous. He rushes across the hall to the bathroom. What would she do? Wouldn't she wait for him to come back, to find out how sick he was? What she actually did was hurry around to the ladies' room and rinse out the glasses."

"You are assuming he was nauseous and told her so,"

said Mrs. Roosevelt. "Isn't it possible he simply excused himself to go to the bathroom?"

"The witnesses say she was in quite a hurry to get to the ladies' room and rinse those glasses."

"That's a highly subjective judgment," said Mrs. Roosevelt.

Kennelly shrugged. "I have enough evidence to hold her on suspicion of murder."

"An important element of your case is missing, you know."

"I know. Motive. While I hold her in jail, she won't be busy hiding or destroying the evidence of her motive."

"If she plotted this murder, she would have hidden or destroyed that evidence already," said Mrs. Roosevelt.

"Well, maybe I'll get a confession."

"You . . . won't interrogate her . . . rigorously?"

Kennelly grinned. "You mean will I beat her with a rubber hose? No, Ma'am, I won't do that. But I am going to hold her—to prevent her from taking it on the lam, if for no other reason."

Mrs. Roosevelt sighed. "I believe she's asking to see me."

"Right. I'll take you back to see her."

Although it was well after midnight, Thérèse Rolland lay awake on the cot in her cell, smoking a cigarette and staring at the ceiling. Seeing Mrs. Roosevelt outside, she started, as if she could not believe who it was. She scrambled off the cot, tossed the cigarette in the toilet, and stepped to the bars.

"I didn't think you would come yet tonight," she whispered hoarsely. "It must be— What time *is* it?"

"A little after midnight," said the First Lady. "There is

nothing much we can do about your situation tonight, but I wanted you to know I am here and am concerned."

Thérèse Rolland was a woman of thirty years, maybe thirty-five. Her hair was red: bright, flaming red. Her white skin was heavily freckled, not only on her face but on her arms as well. Her eyes were pale blue. Her eyebrows were red, but her lashes were blonde and so light they were hardly visible. She was small, no more than five feet two, but her slight figure was womanly. She wore a gray cotton dress, short-sleeved, with a square yoke, the skirt awkwardly short, barely reaching her knees: the uniform of the jail.

She gripped the cell bars and pressed her forehead to them. "I am sufferin' a horrible nightmare," she said.

"Are you innocent?"

"I swear I am, Mrs. Roosevelt," she said. She was from Louisiana and spoke with a southern accent. "I swear. Why in the world would I want Paul dead? He was my *friend*!"

"Terry . . . I will see to it that a good lawyer comes to see you," said Mrs. Roosevelt.

Thérèse Rolland shook her head. "I don't know what he can do. That police detective believes I'm guilty! He just . . . He just right off decided I killed Paul, and he brought me in here and locked me up! It's the awfulest thing ever happened to anybody!"

She sobbed. She used the back of her hand to wipe away tears. "Mrs. Roosevelt! Isn't there any way I can get out of here? My father and mother find out I'm in jail, it'll *kill* 'em."

"I'll do what I can for you, Terry," said the First Lady.

II

By the time Mrs. Roosevelt stopped in to pay her usual morning call on the President he had already seen the story in the *Washington Post*—

MURDER AT WHITE HOUSE

Woman Staffer Charged in

Poisoning Death

Thérèse (Terry) Rolland, 33, is being held without bail in the District jail, charged with murder in the cyanide poisoning of Paul L. Duroc, 40. Both are members of the White House staff. The alleged poisoning occurred about seven o'clock Wednesday evening on the second floor of the Executive (West) Wing.

According to police, Duroc collapsed and died in the men's room, having rushed there complaining of nausea. Dr. Gabriel Hupp, physician on duty at the White House last evening, was summoned. On examining Duroc, Dr. Hupp

17

immediately recognized the symptoms of potassium cyanide poisoning. Emergency measures to save the stricken man were of no avail, and Duroc died within a few minutes.

Police have declined to comment as to exactly what evidence they have to support the charge against Miss Rolland, except to say that she was alone with Duroc in his office for some time before he collapsed and that the two were drinking bourbon.

WHITE HOUSE: NO COMMENT

The office of the President's Press Secretary said it had "no comment" on the death and the murder charge. When the President retired last night, he had not been informed of the death or of the arrest. Mrs. Roosevelt was away from the White House on a speaking engagement and had not been informed.

Paul L. Duroc, formerly a professor of accountancy at Tulane University, also formerly a member of the Louisiana legislature, was regarded as something of a protégé of the late Senator Huey Long. His appointment to the White House staff was undoubtedly a political bow to Senator Long. His official title was Deputy Assistant to the President. His function was to conduct surprise audits of government offices and departments, looking for waste or corruption. His 1935 audit of the Rural Electrification Administration resulted in the resignation of Administrator David Elliott.

Paul Duroc was born in New Orleans in 1896. He was a graduate of Tulane University and the Harvard Business School. He was unmarried.

Thérèse Rolland, called Terry, is also from New Orleans and is also a protégé of Huey Long. She came to Washington in 1934 and was appointed White House purchasing agent. It has been her duty to seek bids and obtain the best prices on everything purchased for use at the White House, from food and drink to office equipment and supplies.

She was publicly complimented by Mrs. Roosevelt a few months ago for having saved substantial money on the purchase of the uniforms worn by White House ushers and maids. Traditionally, these uniforms were custom-made, as are the uniforms of the staff at wealthy English houses. Special piping, buttons, and fabrics were specified, to afford the ushers and maids a distinctive White House style. Miss Rolland recommended that the staff dress in off-the-shelf uniforms, such as might be worn by the staff of a wealthy American home or the staff of a hotel. This recommendation was accepted, and the saving resulted.

The detective in charge of the investigation is Lieutenant Edward Kennelly. Although he declined to release any further information last night, it has been learned that Miss Rolland emphatically denies the charge of murder.

"I suppose this will have your attention," the President said to Mrs. Roosevelt, tapping a finger on the newspaper story.

"They've not proved a case against the poor young woman. I shall at least see to it that a competent lawyer visits her and takes charge of her defense."

"It might be well if you limit yourself to that," he said. "Be careful, Babs. Be careful. A thing like this could become a big embarrassment."

Mrs. Roosevelt went from the President's bedroom downstairs to the small dining room. The President was receiving Professor Albert Einstein in the Oval Office at ten, to meet with a small group of men who had constituted themselves an unofficial science advisory committee. Learning that

Professor Einstein's train from New Jersey would arrive about eight and that Mrs. Einstein was accompanying him, the First Lady had sent an invitation for the Einsteins to join her for breakfast. While the professor was with the President, she would escort Mrs. Einstein on a tour of the White House.

New York Mayor Fiorello La Guardia was in Washington that week, meeting with members of Congress; and he, too, had asked for a breakfast meeting with the First Lady. Mrs. Roosevelt had decided it would be interesting to put these contrasting legendary characters together over an intimate breakfast. She had been looking forward to it all week.

The ebullient mayor was in the hall waiting for her when Mrs. Roosevelt came off the elevator. Literally bouncing on his feet, he rushed toward her, hand extended.

"Eleanor! Thanks for asking me!"

Mayor La Guardia was not nearly as tall as the First Lady—which didn't bother him; he was not as tall as most people. His face split in a wide grin.

"It's good to see you, Mayor," she said.

"The Einsteins are in the Blue Room."

She went to the Blue Room and introduced herself to Professor Einstein and Mrs. Einstein. Then she introduced Mayor La Guardia. She led the breakfast party across the hall and into the private dining room.

Professor Albert Einstein was an easily recognized and unforgettable figure. He was known for his crown of long, unruly white hair, also for his tall forehead, his wide sad eyes, and for the mustache that had remained dark after his hair turned white. He was wearing a dark gray suit with vest, a stiff wing collar, and a loosely knotted black necktie.

His wife was a gray-haired woman with narrow eyes, wearing a pink-and-white cameo on her blouse.

The conversation over breakfast was bland, even stilted. The Einsteins spoke with heavy German accents. The talk livened when Mrs. Roosevelt encouraged Mrs. Einstein to say something about the experiences in Germany that had led her and her husband to decide to live permanently in the United States.

"In the night," said Mrs. Einstein. "They come. *Sturmabteilungers.* Storm troopers. They have said we are hiding arms for the Communists. All night they search, while we sit on the bed. Every floor, every room, they open everything. After all this, they find a weapon and take it away. It was the knife we use to slice bread!"

"Four times," said the professor. "Four times we are searched."

"That guy Hitler is a real louse," said Mayor La Guardia. "A real louse."

"Louse . . . ?" asked Mrs. Einstein.

"A little bug that causes an itch," said the mayor.

"Ah, yes," said Mrs. Einstein.

A few minutes later the mayor handed Professor Einstein a small piece of paper on which he had earlier written an algebra problem. "That," he said. "That almost ended my education. I struggled with that for hours, thought I was going to flunk math if I couldn't solve that."

Professor Einstein smiled. He took a fountain pen from his vest pocket and began to scratch numbers on the paper. His neat, spidery mathematical handwriting was unique, recognized everywhere. In a moment he handed the paper back, equation solved.

"Better than an autograph," said La Guardia as he folded

the paper and returned it to his pocket. "I'll have that framed and hang it in my office."

"You send to me an autograph, too," said Einstein. "A picture of you wearing your fire hat. I'll hang it in my office."

La Guardia was flattered and grinned again. "Professor," he said, "they tell me you have a short explanation for relativity, so simple even the man who couldn't do that algebra problem can understand it. Is that so?"

Einstein nodded. "Yes. Think of it this way. When you sit with a pretty girl for two hours, you think it has only been one minute. When you sit on a hot stove for one minute, you think it has been two hours. That is relativity."

It was after eleven before Mrs. Roosevelt could get away from the White House and go to District police headquarters. Since it would have been difficult for her to avoid being seen and recognized in the visitors' room of the jail, Lieutenant Kennelly took her back to the cells again.

Terry Rolland looked as if she had not slept. When Mrs. Roosevelt took her hand, the young woman leaned limply against the bars and sighed.

"I have called an attorney and asked him to come see you," said Mrs. Roosevelt. "His name is John Evans. He is a fine, competent trial lawyer, and I am sure he will be of great help to you."

Terry Rolland's voice was weak. She asked, "How do they execute people in the District? By electrocution? Or hangin'?"

"If you are innocent, you are not going to be hanged *or* electrocuted. You must fix your attention on your defense."

"I have to think about it."

"Terry . . . Tell me something. What did Paul Duroc say to you just before he left his office and went to the bathroom?"

"He said, 'Excuse me. I have to go to the bathroom.' Somethin' like that."

"Did he say he felt ill?"

Terry Rolland shook her head. "No. He didn't say nothin'. I had no idea he was ill."

"Do you understand why Lieutenant Kennelly thinks you are guilty of murder?"

"He interrogated me for an hour and a half last night. I think I understand what he was drivin' at."

"Terry, you must understand. Paul Duroc died of cyanide poisoning. Once he had swallowed the poison, he had to collapse within a minute or so; no one can remain erect and conscious for longer than that, having been poisoned with cyanide. That means he had to have swallowed the poison while you were with him. The bottle of bourbon from which the two of you were drinking has been examined, and there is no cyanide in it. It must have been in the glass from which he drank, and you rinsed the two glasses out before anyone could examine them. That is why Lieutenant Kennelly thinks you killed Paul Duroc."

The tiny red-haired woman shrugged disconsolately. "I can think of two possible explanations," she said.

"I should like to hear them."

"First, that he killed himself. Second, that he meant to kill me."

"The witnesses from the West Wing describe you as having been in a great hurry to rinse out those glasses."

Terry Rolland shook her head. "What's a hurry? It was

after seven o'clock. I wanted to go home. I didn't know he was so sick."

"Witnesses say you and Mr. Duroc often closed his office door and had a drink or two together at that time of day."

Terry nodded. "Yes. We often ended the workday by havin' a drink together in his office. Just before we left. We never drank when there was work yet to do. I'd phone him first, and if it was okay I'd go over to the West Wing and up to his office. Usually what we did while we had some bourbon was talk about old times with the senator."

The First Lady, who was wearing the rose-colored dress she had worn to breakfast with Professor Einstein, was wearing white gloves. She closed one gloved hand around a bar of Terry Rolland's cell. "I don't mean to be your interrogator," she said. "I am most skeptical about the charge against you and would like to help you. Do you mind if I ask some additional questions? I have had a little experience with investigations."

"I am happy to know you are helpin' me. No one else is."

"Not many people know you are here, perhaps. You have friends."

"I am going to need them."

Mrs. Roosevelt paused for a moment to study Terry Rolland's place of imprisonment. It was as grim and depressing a thing as she had ever seen: a cell some eight feet deep and perhaps twelve feet wide, brick wall in the rear, brick floor, solid steel walls to either side, bars in front. The only furniture was a narrow iron cot, a toilet with no wooden seat, and a basin with one tap. The walls and bars had been painted an off-white, probably many years ago, and much of the paint had chipped off, leaving the surfaces with a rough and blotchy look. There was no light. All the light came in through the bars, from bare bulbs on the ceiling of the corridor.

The First Lady had glanced at the other women imprisoned in this row of cells. Terry Rolland was the only white woman. The Negro women in the three other occupied cells had barely glanced up as Mrs. Roosevelt walked past. They were lethargic, despondent; they had abandoned hope.

"I have to ask a few questions about your relationship with Mr. Duroc," said the First Lady.

"We were friends," said Terry. "We had known each other in New Orleans. The senator recommended us to the President. We were not intimate."

"That will be asked."

"That is the answer," said Terry.

"Did you see each other away from the White House? I mean, did you go to dinner together or anything like that?"

"Yes. But we didn't sleep together."

"The missing element in this case," said Mrs. Roosevelt, "is motive. Can you think of anything that anyone might discover that could be interpreted as motive for you to kill Mr. Duroc?"

Terry shook her head. "What possible advantage could there be for me to have Paul dead?"

"Think about it. What could someone find out that— Supposing a wholly unreasonable, fanciful interpretation . . . What could someone discover?"

The slight young woman turned away from the bars and walked the three steps to the rear wall of the cell. She put her hands flat on the painted bricks and shifted her weight to her arms and hands. She shook her head.

"Let me give you a word of encouragement, then," said

Mrs. Roosevelt. "Lieutenant Kennelly is an honest man. I have worked with him before. He will not fabricate a case against you."

Terry returned to the bars. "Maybe he doesn't have to. A jury might send me to . . . to the gallows, just on the basis of the facts he has. Worse has happened."

"Terry. The vial in which the poison was carried to Mr. Duroc's office was found in his wastebasket."

"With my fingerprints on it, you are about to tell me."

"No. With no fingerprints at all on it. It had been handled with gloves, I imagine."

"Well, I had no gloves. My purse was searched. I was stripped naked to be searched, here last night. I had no gloves. Lieutenant Kennelly will have to admit that."

"Well . . . Mr. Evans will be here this afternoon. The lawyer."

Terry gripped the bars tight in her fists. "When my daddy finds out I'm in jail, it's gonna *kill* him. He's got *pride*, a lot of Louisiana-type pride."

"Is there anything I can send you?"

"Well . . . If I'm gonna be sittin' in here, day after day, I'd like to have some books to read. Maybe a book of crossword puzzles. Somethin' to kill the time."

"I'll send those things."

"I'm grateful for your concern. A person locked up in jail is helpless, you know. I can't do anything to get me out of this mess. I have to depend on somebody outside."

Mrs. Roosevelt nodded. "I'll do what I can for you, Terry."

The young woman began to cry. The First Lady patted her hand consolingly and left.

* * *

From the jail, Mrs. Roosevelt went to a luncheon being held by a delegation of wives of members and officers of United Automobile Workers of America.

She was seated at the head table and found herself at the left of Walter Reuther, the young, red-haired labor leader.

"You're going to have to be more careful," he said to her wryly. "According to Winchell, you were to have breakfast with a Communist—Professor Einstein—and here you are having lunch with another one." He shook his head. "The first thing you know, somebody's going to be calling you names."

With the National Labor Relations Act now a part of the law, the UAW was determined to organize the nation's automobile manufacturing plants. That was the chief reason Reuther was in Washington: to win the support of other major unions.

"It won't be easy, will it?" Mrs. Roosevelt asked Reuther.

"The hardest nut to crack will be Ford," said Reuther. "Old Henry is— Well, what is he? Insane? And he's got that murderous thug Harry Bennett for his union-buster."

"The difficulty with Mr. Ford is that he thinks he's infallible," said Mrs. Roosevelt quietly, so no one but Reuther would hear her. "Any man who thinks he is incapable of making a mistake is, of course, insane—in a sense, at least."

"Saint Henry," muttered Reuther, shaking his head. "But I tell you one thing for sure, Mrs. Roosevelt. We *are going* to unionize the Ford Motor Company, whether the old man likes it or not."

The First Lady nodded thoughtfully.

"Do you have any idea what Ford workers have to put up with?" Reuther asked. "Besides low wages for backbreaking work on a fast assembly line, they have to put up with surprise 'visits' to their homes by Ford security men. They're not supposed to drink, and company cops look into their iceboxes to see if they have any beer. Of course"—he grinned and shrugged—"they do get free dancing lessons."

"What's that?"

"Ford employees get free dancing lessons. Old Henry thinks ballroom dancing is a good, healthy thing for people to do, so he gives his workers free dancing lessons. The men and women in the office building are actually *compelled* to learn to dance and attend company-sponsored dances."

"I have heard," said Mrs. Roosevelt, "that Mr. Bennett has set up a target and fires his pistol in his office."

"That is true," said Walter Reuther. "And Harry Bennett's got a bullet with the name Walter Reuther scratched on it."

Sandra Wilson, Paul Duroc's secretary, had not come to the White House on Thursday. She had been in an office adjoining his when he crossed the hall to the men's room. Although she was a witness, probably an important witness, she was so distraught on Wednesday night that Kennelly felt he should let her go home.

Mrs. Roosevelt suggested to Szczygiel that the young woman would be more comfortable giving her statement in the First Lady's study, rather than in a Secret Service office or at police headquarters. So it was arranged. Szczygiel brought her over from the West Wing. Kennelly was not there yet.

Sandra Wilson was a plump, bosomy girl, no more than nineteen, wearing a dark-blue knit dress stretched tight over her ample figure. She was a natural blonde, but her hair had been stripped of color and curled to emulate the style of the actress Jean Harlow.

Mrs. Roosevelt could not recall ever having seen her before. "How long have you worked in the White House, dear?" she asked when the girl had sat down.

"About six months, Ma'am," said Sandra nervously.

"Have you ever been in the White House proper before, Miss Wilson?"

"Well, they take new employees on a tour of the big rooms downstairs."

"I don't want to ask you any questions about last evening until Lieutenant Kennelly of the District police arrives," said Mrs. Roosevelt, "but I do want you to be comfortable here and not feel that you are under any pressure."

Tears came to the girl's eyes, and she wiped them away with the back of her hand. "Mr. Duroc was a wonderful man," she whispered. "What a terrible, gruesome way to die!"

"Have you worked for Mr. Paul Duroc all the time you've been here?"

Sandra nodded.

"Would you like a cup of coffee, dear? Or tea?"

"No, thank you."

"Well, I am going to have some coffee brought. I know Mr. Szczygiel and Lieutenant Kennelly will have some. Maybe you'll change your mind."

Kennelly arrived a minute or so later.

"We've waited for you, Lieutenant," said the First Lady. "We've asked almost nothing of Miss Wilson. Would you like to begin, or shall I?"

"You do it, Ma'am. I'll stick in other questions when I have some."

"Well then, dear," said Mrs. Roosevelt to Sandra Wilson. "Suppose you tell us what you remember about the events of last evening."

The girl sighed. "Miss Rolland came over from the White House about seven. A little before seven. She came over three or four times a week, but usually a little earlier, like maybe six-fifteen or six-thirty. She and Mr. Duroc had drinks in his office. Usually they left separately. Sometimes they left together. Sometimes he took her to dinner. They always closed the door. Their conversation seemed to be full of jokes. I could hear them laughing in there."

"Did you hear them laughing last evening?"

"Yes. They were in there only about— Oh, less than five minutes, when he opened the door and went across to the men's room. I heard him yell. And then . . . somebody came out of the men's room calling for a doctor."

"How long was he in the men's room before you heard him yell?" asked Kennelly.

"I don't know. Maybe a minute. Probably less."

"Did you see Miss Rolland leave, carrying the glasses?" asked Mrs. Roosevelt.

"Yes."

"Was she in a hurry?"

"Yes."

"Where was she when Mr. Duroc cried out?"

"Probably in the ladies' room."

"In other words," said Mrs. Roosevelt, "she was not still in Mr. Duroc's office when he cried out."

"No, she was gone."

"Was it the usual thing for Miss Rolland to rinse out the glasses after she and Mr. Duroc had their drinks?"

"Yes."

"Mr. Duroc didn't expect *you* to do it?"

"No."

"You didn't have to do housekeeping chores for him?"

"I filled his two thermos bottles every day: one with hot coffee, the other with ice water. So he never sent me out for coffee . . . or anything like that."

Szczygiel had a question. "Did he ever serve drinks to anyone else? I mean, in his office?"

"I think so, occasionally. I know he gave Mr. Hopkins a drink one afternoon."

"Harry Hopkins? Yes, Harry likes bourbon," said Mrs. Roosevelt with a little laugh. "With oysters. Can you believe that? Bourbon and oysters!"

"Who rinsed out the glasses after he served bourbon to Mr. Hopkins?" asked Szczygiel.

"I suppose he must have done it himself," said Sandy. "I didn't do it."

"Did he ever offer *you* a drink?" asked Kennelly.

"Yes, Sir. Just once he did. I don't like bourbon and said no thanks."

"Miss Wilson, can you think of any reason why anyone would want to kill Mr. Duroc?"

The chubby little girl shook her head. "No. Just no reason. He was a *wonderful* man. Why, it was wonderful just to hear him talk: that southern accent . . ." She sobbed. "I can't think of any reason why anybody would want to harm him."

Mrs. Roosevelt took Sandra Wilson to the elevator. When she returned to her study she called for Dr. Hupp. While they waited for him, they talked, she and Szczygiel and Kennelly.

"I can tell you two things about Terry Rolland," said Kennelly. "One is in her favor. The other one isn't."

"Tell us what's in her favor first, if you please," said Mrs. Roosevelt.

Kennelly nodded. "She left no fingerprints on the bourbon bottle. The only prints are his, all over it."

"Of course there were no fingerprints at all on the vial found in the wastebasket," said Szczygiel.

"What is the thing that's bad for her?" asked Mrs. Roosevelt.

"This isn't the first time she's been in jail," said Kennelly. "She served sixty days on a Louisiana prison farm. She pleaded guilty to rigging bids on textbook contracts for the public schools."

"How do you know?"

"FBI fingerprint files."

"Weren't those files checked when she applied for a job at the White House?"

Szczygiel shook his head. "We've pressed for that for years. But no. As a practical matter, all she needed was the endorsement letter from Senator Long."

Mrs. Roosevelt shook her head. "So our White House purchasing agent has been a young woman who served time in prison for dishonest purchasing practices."

"It was six years ago," said Kennelly. "She worked for the State of Louisiana when Huey Long was governor. As soon as she got out of jail, he put her in another state job."

"It must have been damned serious business if Huey could not keep her out of jail," said Szczygiel.

"Not necessarily," said Mrs. Roosevelt. "The Kingfish moved in mysterious ways his purposes to achieve."

"I suppose the next thing you'll say is that she wasn't necessarily guilty," Kennelly grumbled.

"I say, let's not be in too big a hurry to reach a final decision in the case before us," said Mrs. Roosevelt. "I say, let's get more facts about that Louisiana conviction."

"I'll telephone the United States District Attorney in New Orleans," said Szczygiel.

"Please do. Let me know if you find out anything interesting," said Mrs. Roosevelt.

Stan Szczygiel insisted a Secret Service agent must be present whenever D.C. police detectives worked inside the White House. He was with Ed Kennelly as Kennelly directed his team in a thorough search of the West Wing office that had been occupied by Paul Duroc.

They began with the desk. Both of them knew there was a pistol in the center drawer; they had seen it there the night before. Kennelly put a pencil through the trigger guard and lifted the pistol out. He stared at it for a moment before handing it over to the fingerprint man. It was a snub-nose .38 Smith & Wesson.

"I bet it's never been fired, from the look of it," said Kennelly. "Wonder why he kept a gun in his desk?"

"He cost several men their jobs over the past two years," said Szczygiel. "I wonder if he carried it when he left here. He wasn't wearing a shoulder holster last night, was he?"

Kennelly shook his head. "No, but he could've shoved it down in his pants or stuck it in a pocket."

"I don't like it," said Szczygiel. "Finding a pistol we didn't know about this close to the Oval Office. We're going to have to tighten up on this sort of thing."

"I suggest you do," said Kennelly dryly.

Besides the pistol, they found in the drawer a crushed package of Spuds cigarettes with only two cigarettes remaining, several books of paper matches imprinted with the advertising of local restaurants, a bottle of aspirin tablets, a fingernail clipper and a fingernail file, assorted pencils, two boxes of paper clips, a staple puller, and a box of rubber bands. The side drawers contained nothing but files.

"Like a hotel room," said Kennelly. "You can't tell who lives there; it has no mark of anybody's personality. Was this man *anybody*? This desk doesn't suggest anybody."

A small personal address book lay on top of the desk. Szczygiel picked it up. He leafed through it. "Here's the address and phone number for Thérèse Rolland," he said. "Otherwise . . . Government agencies."

Two thermos carafes sat in a tray on the desk. Kennelly unscrewed the cap on one and smelled stale coffee. The other was half full of water. The insulation of the carafe was good enough that the water was still cool. Kennelly made a note to himself to have both carafes sent to the lab.

Kennelly ran his hand along the bottom of the center drawer. "So," he muttered. He shook his head. "Not very original. Not original at all." He showed Szczygiel a key with tape hanging from it. "Taping something to the bottom of a drawer—any burglar worth a nickel will check for that. So will any cop."

The long thin key was a little rusty. The word MOSLER was stamped on both sides of the bow.

"Key to a safe-deposit box," said Kennelly.

"We need a court order to open it."

"Well . . . maybe. That depends on what bank. We can't tell from the key what bank it's from. Mosler is the name of the vault manufacturer—for every bank in Washington, I imagine."

"Even if we knew what bank to go to, we don't know the box is in the name Paul Duroc," said Szczygiel.

Kennelly nodded. "I'd like to know what's in that box," he said. "I'd like to know why he hid the key that way."

They pulled out the remaining drawers and checked the bottoms. Nothing.

They went through a wooden file cabinet and found nothing but files reflecting Duroc's duties as an auditor.

From Duroc's office, they went down to the ground floor of the West Wing and out through the north entrance, into the colonnade that led east past the swimming pool and into the ground floor of the White House proper.

No one had been quite sure where office space should be found for Thérèse Rolland. She had been moved twice during the short time she had worked at the White House. For now, she was installed in a large room on the east end of the ground floor. The room was far too grand for her needs as an office but was furnished anything but grandly. She had a scarred old yellow-oak desk, a wooden swivel chair, and three wooden filing cabinets.

Szczygiel and Kennelly found no pistol in Terry Rolland's desk, but they did find a half-empty bottle of bourbon. They also found a package of Sen-Sen, which she could use to cover the odor of whiskey on her breath. Otherwise, a thorough search of her office turned up nothing suggestive.

"In particular, you did not find any potassium cyanide," said Mrs. Roosevelt.

The two men had come to the First Lady's study on the

second floor to report to her what they had learned by searching the two offices.

"I hardly expected to find potassium cyanide," said Kennelly. "She would be a stupid murderer if she left a supply of the poison in her desk drawer."

"Where does one obtain potassium cyanide, Lieutenant Kennelly?" asked Mrs. Roosevelt. "Is it not difficult to obtain?"

"It *is* difficult to obtain," said Kennelly. "But not impossible. It's used in quite a few industrial processes."

"But it is notorious as a lethal poison," she said. "I assume you cannot just go into your pharmacy and tell the druggist you want an ounce of potassium cyanide."

"No, you can't," Kennelly agreed. "But if you are a laboratory worker, particularly around certain industries, you can get it. You can steal it."

"Miss Rolland is not a laboratory worker."

"You are suggesting," said Kennelly, "that she couldn't have poisoned Duroc because she would have had so much difficulty in getting her hands on the poison. There is an answer to that, Ma'am."

"Which is?"

"*Somebody* got their hands on it. It would be just as tough for anybody who's not a chemist or doesn't work in an industry where they used potassium cyanide. Anyway— *Somebody* got it. *Somebody* used it."

"And Miss Rolland was in the room with Duroc when he drank it," said Szczygiel.

"So you believe she's guilty. Have you found motive?"

Both men shook their heads.

"Well then, Lieutenant Kennelly, do you mind looking into alternatives to Miss Rolland as the murderer?"

"Of course not. Further investigation may strengthen the case against her, you understand."

"I would like to assign an auditor to review the files you found in Mr. Duroc's desk drawer," said Mrs. Roosevelt. "It is possible he may have been investigating something that someone else did not want investigated."

"We're putting special locks on his desk drawers and filing cabinets," said Szczygiel. "And on hers. Whatever is in those files will be there, intact, until your auditor looks at them."

"Good."

Leaving Mrs. Roosevelt's study, Stan Szczygiel and Ed Kennelly walked out into the President's early-evening cocktail hour.

The President always hoped to assemble a few convivial spirits at the end of the day, to share with him two or three drinks and some amiable conversation. Missy LeHand was usually there. Louis Howe had always come, until he no longer could. Pa Watson came, and lately Harry Hopkins. Occasionally, the invitations were politically inspired, as they were today.

The cocktail cart, laden with bottles, glasses, shakers, and ice was wheeled to the West Sitting Hall by Arthur Prettyman. The West Sitting Hall was a part of the family quarters of the White House and was furnished by each First Family, either by new furniture or with things brought from home for their four-year or eight-year stay. The wealthy Hoovers had furnished the room very stylishly. The Roosevelts, whose budget for the purpose was not nearly so great, had furnished it mostly with pieces from their New

York home: comfortable furniture, where the President could comfortably entertain friends.

Missy helped him serve cocktails. He loved to mix martinis—strong ones, five to one—but not all his guests enjoyed that cocktail, so he kept Scotch on hand, and bourbon, as well as sherry for the occasional guest who did not want hard liquor.

The President was amused this afternoon by the odd mix of guests he had invited. Senator Theodore Bilbo of Mississippi had asked for an appointment; and, knowing the senator's affinity for bourbon, the President had suggested he come by at six-thirty. The senator had returned word that he would be delighted. Besides Senator Bilbo, Joseph P. Kennedy had come in. He had come to the White House to bring a few bottles of choice, as he had often done over the years; and he was clever enough to arrive at the hour when he was likely to be asked to stay for the cocktail hour.

Joe Kennedy was a Boston Irishman, appointed by the President to be the first chairman of the SEC. He was immoderately ambitious but intelligent, driving, and effective. It was said of him that he had imported liquor during the Prohibition years, so he was really just a glorified bootlegger. In any event, he was now a wealthy businessman—but a businessman of a new stripe, one who saw the need for social change in the United States: instinctively something of a liberal, certainly not a hidebound conservative.

Senator Bilbo was a Negro-hating racist, an inflammatory orator who played to the lowest instincts of his constituency. He was the kind of man Franklin D. Roosevelt detested. Still, he led a bloc in Congress; and if legislation beneficial to all Americans, including the Negroes, was to be enacted, his bloc could not be scorned. The President had long since given up all hope of winning a degree of moderation from Bilbo but felt he could not refuse to receive him.

Politics did indeed make strange bedfellows. Bilbo could never be more than a regional demagogue, never a threat to make over the United States to his own liking. That had not been true of Huey Long. It was extremely doubtful that the Kingfish would ever have become President of the United States, but it was not impossible; and it was not unlikely he would have had a major, and maybe damaging, influence on the congressional elections of 1936, if not on the presidential election itself. Bilbo, for reasons of his own, had called the Kingfish "that Madman Huey Long" and had worked to counter the spread of Long influence in the Deep South.

When Szczygiel and Kennelly walked out of Mrs. Roosevelt's study, both Kennedy and Bilbo were already with the President. Joseph Kennedy was drinking one of the President's martinis. Missy and the senator were drinking bourbon and water.

"Ah," the President laughed. "Hawkshaw the Detective, Numbers One and Two. Been in conferring with Sherlock Roosevelt, have you? Sit down and have a drink with us. As you gentlemen know, one of our staff is accused of murdering another member of our staff. These fellows, together with my wife, who cannot resist sticking her nib in such things, are the investigative team. Any progress, fellows?"

"The evidence is pretty clear, Mr. President," said Szczygiel.

"Except to my wife, I imagine. She instinctively sympathizes with the accused in all such matters. Sit down. Sit down. At this time of day, all of us are entitled to a little relaxation. If you don't all know each other, you do know who each other are. Senator Bilbo, Joe Kennedy, Stan

Szczygiel of the Secret Service, Ed Kennelly of the D.C. homicide squad."

Joe Kennedy was a sandy-haired Irishman with an intent face and round spectacles that gave him a somewhat owlish aspect. Senator Bilbo was an older man, with a bald dome and a supply of wrinkles that seemed heavy, that seemed to settle toward the bottom of his face and accumulate there.

Kennelly took a bourbon from Missy. Szczygiel, who appreciated gin, pleased the President by taking the last martini from the shaker, making it necessary for the President to shake more.

"We've been *talkin'*, gentlemen, 'bout th' *upcomin'* 'lection," said Senator Bilbo in his drawn-out Mississippi drawl, taking twice as long as anyone else in the room would have taken to speak the same words, but speaking them with careful intonation. "I've got no *fear* but that the Pres'dent is gonna be re-elected. An' *handily.* Handily."

"Tell us about Gerald L. K. Smith, Senator," said the President. "What impact will he have?"

Gerald L. K. Smith was one of a dozen rabble-rousing, Bible-thumping charlatans who had tried to jerk over their own shoulders the mantle of the fallen Kingfish—Smith was attempting to out-Huey Huey. He was a confused amalgam of populist and fascist, and he was joining with Father Coughlin, Dr. Townsend, and others to form a third party for the 1936 presidential election.

"Gerald L. K. Smith," the senator intoned, "is a contemptible, dirty, vicious, pusillanimous, with-malice-afore-thought, damnable, self-made liar!"

The President clapped his hands as he guffawed. "I believe you've covered him, Ted."

A few minutes later, though, the President turned somber as Senator Bilbo spoke of the Negro race—

"They are inferior to us. That's obvious. That's *wholly* obvious. Folks No'th, don't see very many, ought to come down Mississippi way and have a good look at what we're asked to consider *equals.* Why, I'd as soon give the vote to alligators as coons—and figure they'd vote smarter. Way I look at it is this— Folks from Mississippi, we don't come up No'th trying to tell y'all what to do 'bout *your* Nigras. So why you figure you got call to come down South and tell us what to do with *our'n?*"

The President did not answer, did not open an argument in which, he knew, he would be unable to make any points with a man whose mind was set in concrete. "Tell us, Joe," he said to Kennedy. "What do you think about this fellow Churchill and all his talk about Hitler being dangerous?"

III

A few minutes after ten the next morning, Mrs. Roosevelt left the White House and was driven to the Washington flying field just across the river. She had accepted the offer of the Douglas Aircraft Company to be flown on a quick trip to a town in West Virginia. Her interest was in seeing a West Virginia mining town, to become more intimately acquainted with the problems of the miners and their families. The Douglas Aircraft Company wanted her to fly in its new airplane, to get newsreel coverage.

The combination was irresistible to the newsreels—and to newspaper photographers as well. Mrs. Roosevelt on another of her fast tours of inspection, plus a first look at a new airliner!

The new airplane could carry as many as twenty-one passengers, so a few of the cameramen and reporters could come along on the flight.

The pilot met the First Lady in the terminal building. He was a test pilot for Douglas Aircraft, but he assured Mrs.

Roosevelt that the airplane was not experimental but was to go into regular airline service with American Airlines first, then with others, within two or three months.

"What do you call the airplane, Captain Miller?" she asked in a tone that unfortunately suggested a rehearsed speech, as cameras rolled and microphones were thrust toward her.

"We call her the DST, Ma'am—meaning Douglas Sleeper Transport," said the captain, enunciating his words in the same stilted way. "Fourteen passengers can sleep in berths on a transcontinental flight. Set up with seats and no berths, she carries twenty-one. In that configuration, we call her DC-3."

"Well, Captain Miller, I am most anxious to fly to West Virginia now and be back at the White House in time for dinner. Shall we take off?"

The cameras followed the First Lady and the pilot as they walked a few yards across the ramp and approached the big twin-engine transport plane. It was painted with the insignia of Douglas Aircraft, but most of its aluminum remained unpainted and gleamed in the sunlight. The captain took Mrs. Roosevelt's arm as she mounted the three steps and ducked her head to enter the passenger cabin.

This airplane was not set up to carry twenty-one passengers, nor was it compartmented for sleeping. This day it was specially configured with fourteen wide, deeply upholstered seats set in the cabin at an angle so that the passengers sat with their backs to the windows, though they could turn and comfortably look over their shoulders at the landscape below. Captain Miller explained that DC-3s configured like this would be used for special, extra-fare flights.

Mrs. Roosevelt sat in front on the left. Malvina Thompson,

her private and personal secretary, sat across the aisle from her. A Secret Service agent sat behind them. Half a dozen reporters and cameramen sat to the rear.

Within minutes the airplane roared down the runway. As the tail wheel left the pavement, the floor of the cabin leveled; then it tipped again as the DC-3 climbed.

The new airplane was amazingly fast. Once it had reached its cruising altitude of about three thousand feet, it reached a cruising speed of more than two hundred miles per hour. In the course of one hour, it covered a distance that would take an express train at least four hours to cover, an automobile driver six or seven hours, probably longer.

The view was spectacular. The westward course took the plane over the Blue Ridge Mountains, then over the Shenandoah Valley. The captain climbed to four thousand feet as the plane cruised above the forested mountains of eastern West Virginia.

Less than an hour after takeoff the DC-3 circled, dropped over a mountain ridge, and descended fast, with passengers' ears popping, to the runway on the airfield at Elkins, West Virginia.

The newsmen scrambled out first, set up their cameras, and filmed the First Lady, here in the West Virginia mountains by noon, having had her breakfast at the White House.

The governor was there to meet her, the mayor, a congressman, and the leaders of the local Democratic Party. She shook hands, beamed on them all, and hurried as fast as she could to the car that waited to take her to the coal mines.

She allowed the newsmen to cover her greeting on the front porch of a coal miner's home; then she went in alone

with the family, while the state police held the newsmen at
the edge of the junk-littered yard.

Try as she would, her "dinner"—these people had never
heard the word *lunch*—in the home of a West Virginia coal
miner could not be what it would have been if she had not
been there.

In the first place, the man of the house and his eldest son,
also a coal miner, were at home in midday. In the second
place, these two men had scrubbed so long and hard that
the skin of their faces gleamed pink. They wore wrinkled
white shirts, collars buttoned but with no neckties. The man
wore a shiny black suit, the son a pair of pin-striped wool
trousers. The women—wife, two daughters, a daughter-in-
law, and a sister of the husband—wore flowered dresses.

The table was set with platters of chicken and steaming
bowls of potatoes and lima beans, plus hot, fresh-baked
bread with butter.

"It ain't a usual thing for us kind of folks to see the wife
of a President of the United States at our table," the husband said. "Fact, ain't none of us ever seed a President or
a President's wife afore. We know we ain't got the kind of
manners we ought to have, to take our meal with you,
Ma'am. What we got is friendship an' goodwill an' a lotta
respec'."

"And that, Mr. Buckley, is far more important than pol-
ished manners," said Mrs. Roosevelt.

She enjoyed her meal. Genuinely. By the time they had
sat at the table fifteen minutes, the family relaxed; and she
was able to draw from them some account of how people
lived in this part of the country.

Later, they showed her.

The Buckleys, she guessed, lived better than most of their

neighbors. Mrs. Buckley showed her the kitchen. To cook, she burned coal in an iron stove. A big round basin sat on a table shoved against the wall. That was the kitchen sink. Two white-enamel buckets contained the water Mrs. Buckley used for cooking and washing dishes. Hot water could be dipped from a tank in the stove. All the water came from a well in the back yard. The kitchen floor had once been covered with blue-and-white linoleum. Only fragments of it remained, so most of the floor was crude lumber with wide cracks between boards.

The house was lighted with oil lamps, heated by the kitchen stove and a coal-burning stove in the living room. Mr. and Mrs. Buckley slept in a simple iron double bed that occupied about a third of the living room. The rest of the family—adult son and his tiny pregnant wife, two daughters, and the sister-in-law—shared the unheated second floor, where only the son and daughter-in-law had the privacy of a couple of blankets nailed to the ceiling. The others slept in two beds in a single open room.

She walked a few yards up what was called "th' holler" and met Mrs. Buckley's mother, a thin, stringy, yellow-haired woman who lived alone in a one-room shack. Something the size of a golf ball was growing on the old lady's throat, just ahead of and beneath her left ear. Obviously she couldn't afford the surgery necessary to remove it, and Mrs. Roosevelt wondered if it was something that would kill her. She realized, too, after a few minutes, that the woman she had thought of as an old lady was at least five years younger than herself.

Only one of the photographers took a picture of the woman. He was interested only in photographing her hands as she wove a basket. She sold her baskets—"good, lasty ones," she assured Mrs. Roosevelt—to earn money. She presented one as a gift, but Mrs. Roosevelt insisted on paying her a dollar for it. The photographer bought one, too.

In the course of the next hour she visited the homes of three more miners and found that, as she had suspected, the Buckleys lived better than most.

"But a man don' live t' ole age at it, y' see," said one of the women. "Us buries 'em. Th' mine, it takes it out of a man. Somethin' in th' work jus' wearies 'em out."

Next, Mrs. Roosevelt was driven to a minehead. No miners were coming up or going down at that hour. A representative of the mine operator explained that it took half an hour to lift one of the multicar elevators out of the mine and that the elevators only ran on shift changes. If a man went down at the beginning of a shift, he had to stay down to the end.

"It's steady work, you know," he explained to the First Lady. "Many of our men are sons, grandsons, and great-grandsons of men who went to work here just after the Civil War. It gets to be a family tradition with them."

She boarded the DC-3 before four that afternoon and was back at the White House before six.

While Mrs. Roosevelt was traveling to West Virginia and back, Stan Szczygiel and Ed Kennelly searched the homes of Terry Rolland and Paul Duroc.

Like most young women who worked for the government in those days, Terry lived in a boardinghouse. Lieutenant Kennelly presented his warrant to the owner of the house, a Mrs. Dugan, who only glanced at the warrant, nodded, and led the two men upstairs to Terry Rolland's room.

Terry occupied the best room in the huge Victorian

house: a big, sunny corner bedroom on the front of the house, the only room with a private bath. It was handsomely furnished with a four-poster mahogany bed with frilled canopy, a matching chest of drawers and bureau with mirror, and a black-horsehair-covered Victorian settee. She had a radio and a Victrola, the latter one of the new models with an electric drive that you didn't have to wind. A somewhat worn but still elegant Oriental rug covered most of the floor.

Szczygiel looked through the stack of records beside her Victrola. He recognized "Inka Dinka Doo" by Jimmy Durante, "I Got It Bad, and That Ain't Good" with the Duke Ellington Orchestra, "Eadie Was a Lady" by Ethel Merman, and "Minnie the Moocher" by Cab Calloway. Also, she had a record of "Every Man a King," sung by Huey Long.

On an impulse, Szczygiel put the Long record on the turntable. The voice of the late senator, filled with enthusiasm and backed by an orchestra, rang out—

> *Ev'ry man a king! Ev'ry man a king!*
> *For you can be a millionaire!*

Several books lay around. Terry Rolland was apparently a reader—and of some prominent authors, too: Faulkner, Hemingway, Lewis, Wharton, Fitzgerald. She had magazines: *Colliers, Saturday Evening Post, Literary Digest.*

Kennelly, meanwhile, was going through the drawers of her bureau and dresser, finding nothing except a woman's very private things. Someone had remarked to him once that it must be a thrill for a man to search through a woman's underwear. He had replied that someone who hadn't done it couldn't possibly imagine how far from a thrill it was. If he had to do it, he said, his chief hope was that at least everything he had to paw through had been laundered since last worn.

He looked at the labels inside her clothes. New Orleans stores. Some Washington. She was careful about her spending. The labels Trimline and BetterMade said she bought some of her clothes at Sears, Roebuck.

Except for a red rubber enema bag hanging on the wall above her toilet, he found nothing unusual in her bathroom. She washed her face with Cuticura soap, a cake of which lay on her basin, and bathed with bright red Lifebuoy ("Only Lifebuoy fights bee-eee-eee-eee-OH!"). She washed her hair with Mulsified Cocoanut Oil Shampoo and brushed her teeth with Ipana.

"Something interesting here," said Szczygiel. He had dumped the contents of her wastebasket on the floor. "Looka these."

Half a dozen small sheets of notepaper. The notes were cryptic—if, that is, you hadn't used the same code yourself—

HI 4 3 $10
GU 7 6 $10
BE 2 7 $10

The notes meant she had bet ten dollars each on the number three horse in the fourth race at Hialeah, the number six horse in the seventh at Gulfstream, and the number seven horse in the second at Belmont.

She had made the bets by telephone, of course, and had kept notes on her bets.

"If these are one day's, that's a lot of money for a government girl," said Szczygiel.

Kennelly nodded. "We'll take those slips for evidence. What else?"

"What you'd figure. *Racing Form*."

"I'd give a lot," said Kennelly, "to know who she called, who her bookie was. We've got the little notepad she carried in her purse. I'll have any phone numbers in there checked. What've we got for a home phone book?"

Most boardinghouse rooms did not have a private telephone line. This one did. A black French-style telephone instrument sat on the nightstand by the bed. Under it was a D.C. telephone directory. A dozen telephone numbers were penciled on the cover and early pages. Kennelly put it in the middle of the bed with the betting slips—things he meant to take.

Sitting by the telephone, not hidden at all, she had a half-full bottle of Old Granddad's and a small glass. Doubting that either of them would show a trace of potassium cyanide, Kennelly put them on the bed, too.

That was all they found. She bet on the horses. She drank alone in her room.

Mrs. Dugan was a taciturn woman who would say only that Terry Rolland had been a good tenant: quiet, clean, prompt with her rent. She had eaten most of her meals with the other boarders in the boardinghouse dining room.

"Her rent's paid for March. You can tell her the room is hers to the end of the month. I won't change anything."

Paul Duroc had lived in one half of a small brick double house on Columbia Road, near enough to the National Zoo that in the house you could hear the big cats roaring. Five minutes after they entered, Kennelly and Szczygiel discovered that he had not lived here alone. A woman's clothes shared his closet and dresser. Her toiletries took more space in the bathroom than his did.

Szczygiel noted four perfume atomizers, two in the bathroom, two in the bedroom. The names on perfume bottles meant nothing to him, but he recognized that all these tiny bottles of precious liquids had been imported from France. She had boxes of powder, each with a puff. The bath oil and bubble bath in bottles on the rim of the tub were in odd contrast to the chipped enamel of the bathtub.

The clothing in the closet and dresser did not suggest a frugal woman. She wore silk tap panties: what had replaced the bloomers young women had worn for years. Tap panties still had vestigial legs, slit at the sides to the hips. They were thin and loose. She favored lace-trimmed crepe de chine teddies, tea-pink or black—or maybe Duroc favored them and bought them for her. A pair of black Chinese silk pajama bottoms shared a hanger with a black silk bandeau, intimating that the two were worn together, perhaps with nothing else. A blue-and-white nightgown was so sheer it would have concealed nothing.

The daytime clothes—her dresses, skirts, blouses—looked cheap in comparison with her intimate things. The two men could guess that Duroc had bought the intimate things for her, as gifts, and her pedestrian clothing she had bought for herself.

The house was not as well furnished as was Terry's room. The furniture was older, cheaper, worn. Packs of two brands of cigarettes lay on the table by the easy chair: Spuds and Luckies. In the smoking stand lay two amber-colored meerschaum pipes. A tin of Prince Albert tobacco lay at hand. The ashtray in the smoking stand was full, as was the one on the table.

In the kitchen, a bottle of bourbon and one of Scotch sat on the table. The ice in the icebox had all melted. The food was growing warm and would soon spoil. The pan underneath had overflowed. On the back porch a small, rounded cake of ice lay in a spreading spot of water: ice that had been delivered and not brought inside.

"Whoever she is, she heard about his death and lammed," said Kennelly.

"Casual, maybe, but not temporary," said Szczygiel. "She had settled in here. Her clothes are here. Her cosmetics. She *lived* here."

"Right. So— We'd better get the fingerprint boys in," said Kennelly. "Be careful what you touch."

They spent half an hour going through every drawer in every room in the house, looking for a clue to the origin of the safe-deposit box key they had found in Duroc's office. They turned the pictures on the walls, looking for anything he might have taped on the backs.

In the top drawer of the bureau in the bedroom lay a yellow telegram, bearing the date September 8, 1935—

HUEY SHOT THIS EVENING IN CAPITOL ROTUNDA STOP WOUND SERIOUS
BUT PROBABLY NOT FATAL STOP CONDUCT YOURSELF AS IF IT IS FATAL
STOP GET THIS WORD TO TL IMMEDIATELY STOP

O.K.

The time of the telegram showed that someone named O.K. in Baton Rouge, had thought Paul Duroc and whoever TL was should know of the shooting of Huey Long within twenty minutes after it happened.

"TL?" Kennelly asked.

"I don't know," said Szczygiel. "Were there any other Longs in Washington?"

"Mean anything? Make any difference?"

"I think we have to let Mrs. Roosevelt make a judgment on that."

Also in that drawer was Duroc's checkbook. It showed a balance in his checking account of $128.15.

Douglas Aircraft received all the press and newsreel attention it could have wished when the First Lady, having left the White House in mid-morning, returned there in time for dinner, in time for the President's cocktail hour, in fact— having flown all the way to West Virginia and back. As the airline flacks told the reporters repeatedly, this flight had been no stunt by an adventuresome woman accompanying a bold pilot but had been the kind of flight that would become routine within months. Why, she could have eaten meals aboard the plane, if she wanted. A berth could have been set up for her to sleep. This was what airline travel was going to be like.

Back at the White House, Mrs. Roosevelt found a telegram from the Baltimore & Ohio Railroad—

WOULD LIKE MOST RESPECTFULLY TO POINT OUT THAT OUR NATIONAL LIMITED CARRIES PASSENGERS IN ASSURED SAFETY AND SPACIOUS COMFORT BETWEEN WASHINGTON AND ST LOUIS STOP THE LINE PASSES THROUGH WESTERN VIRGINIA WEST VIRGINIA OHIO INDIANA AND ILLI-NOIS STOP SCHEDULES ARRANGED SO THAT TRAVELERS COVER LONG DISTANCES DURING NIGHT HOURS STOP ELEGANT MEALS ARE SERVED BY ATTENTIVE PERSONNEL STOP PRIVATE COMPARTMENTS ARE AVAIL-

ABLE STOP QUICK TRANSFERS AND EFFICIENT SERVICE AVAILABLE TO
OUT OF WAY TOWNS OFF MAIN LINE STOP WOULD APPRECIATE OPPOR-
TUNITY TO SERVE YOU AT AN EARLY DATE WHEN YOU HAVE OCCASION
TO TRAVEL WEST STOP

Other telegrams, from other railroads, invited her to consider travel aboard the Broadway Limited, the Flying Yan-
kee, the Silver Meteor, the California Zephyr, the Chief, the
Super-Chief, and the Sunset Limited.

A telegram from the Burlington Line pointed out that its
Denver Zephyr regularly averaged more than eighty miles
an hour on its run from Chicago to Denver and sometimes
exceeded one hundred miles an hour.

IN ABSOLUTE SAFETY STOP WITH SILVER AND CHINA ON WHITE LINEN
STOP NO RISK OR ADVENTURE STOP TRAVEL IN SECURITY AND COMFORT
WITH PERSONAL PRIVACY STOP FOR ANOTHER HUNDRED MILES AN
HOUR YOU RISK YOUR LIFE IN AN AIRPLANE STOP WHAT IS MORE
RAILROAD TRAVEL IS IMPORTANT TO OUR NATIONS ECONOMY STOP
SUPPORT THE RAILROADS THAT ARE ESSENTIAL TO ECONOMIC HEALTH
NOT THE AIRLINES THAT ARE A ROMANTIC FAD STOP

Thursday's *Chicago Tribune* waited, with a signed edito-
rial by Colonel McCormick—

Having sat down to breakfast with a brilliant scientist who
is suspected by responsible authorities of Communist lean-
ings, Our Eleanor went on to dinner the same evening with
a known and admitted Communist, Walter Reuther, hood-
lum of the United Automobile Workers. We look forward to
Inauguration Day, 1937, when the White House may be
fumigated, the Commies turned out once and for all, and the

Squire of Dutchess County and his loony-bird wife returned to New York where such foolishness is tolerated.

New York tolerates Rooseveltism. America does not. Let the nation be returned to its solid and respectable leaders. Enough! Enough!

IV

In 1936, America was still a land of the six-day work week. This was true at the White House as much as anywhere else. On Saturday morning the President wheeled himself to the Oval Office as early as he did on any other day of the week, and he would remain at his desk just as long.

The First Lady was driven to a breakfast meeting of the Executive Board of the National Association for the Advancement of Colored People, held in the dining room of a modest hotel called the Abraham—a "colored hotel" on the east side of the city. She was guest of honor and made a short speech, after which she left the board to do its business.

Back at the White House before ten, she sat down in her office and placed a telephone call to George Washington University, to the department of chemistry. The White House operator reached a Professor Whipple.

"Mrs. Roosevelt? I'm sorry that Chairman Drake is not in this morning. My name is William Whipple. I'm a professor of chemistry. Is there any way I can help you?"

"I believe there may be, Professor. I suspect you know that a man was murdered in the Executive Wing Wednesday evening. He was poisoned."

"I did read that. Potassium cyanide, was it not?"

"Yes. It has occurred to me that the ordinary person would experience great difficulty trying to obtain that chemical, it being known as a deadly poison. I wonder if you could enlighten me?"

"We keep a small quantity of it on hand in the university laboratories, to use to illustrate certain chemical reactions. It is kept under lock and key, however, and only faculty members, not students, are allowed access to it."

"I understand it is used in certain industrial processes," said Mrs. Roosevelt. "Metallurgy, as I understand. Is there any kind of *small* business that might use it?"

"Only one comes to mind," said Professor Whipple. "It is one of very few chemicals that can dissolve gold and silver. It is sometimes used in small quantities in shops where gold or silver items are restored. An old and badly scuffed piece of gold jewelry, for example, can often be restored to its original luster by immersing it in a bath of potassium cyanide. The chemical will dissolve a tiny quantity of the gold on the surface, exposing fresh gold underneath."

"Are there shops in Washington that do this kind of work?" she asked.

"I don't know of any personally, but I should think there are. Scarred silver pieces are also treated that way. You know, silver can be cleaned—that is, the tarnish taken off—but a silver bowl with an abraded surface, a pattern of tiny, shallow scratches, can be made to gleam again. A few jewelry stores, even a pawnshop here and there, might offer the service."

"And where would such a store obtain potassium cyanide?" she asked.

"Chemical supply houses. We obtain ours from a company in New Jersey. They wouldn't sell potassium cyanide to just anyone, but they do sell to university chemical laboratories and to businesses that can show they have some proper use for it."

"I am grateful to you, Professor. You have been more than helpful."

Her first appointment was with Allen Layman, the auditor from the Treasury Department whom she had asked to look through the files in Paul Duroc's office to see if anything he had been working on afforded any suggestion as to why he had been murdered.

"I asked for an appointment with you as soon as I came across anything I thought might be of interest to you," said Layman. "I'm not finished by any means, but I did find something you might want to know about."

Allen Layman, she judged, had to be well past retirement age. From the loose lids of his watery blue eyes, from his white hair and the deep wrinkles in his face, she took him for a man of seventy or more. He was, however, still straight, square, vigorous, and incisive of conversation.

"What did you find, Mr. Layman?"

"Among the files in his desk was one pertaining to the purchasing office run by Miss Rolland. It contains nothing I could call evidence of any irregularities in her operation. On the other hand, there is a memorandum in it that I thought you should see."

Layman handed her a sheet of printed memorandum paper. The brief memo was typed—

MEMORANDUM

To: Self   Date: 2/11/36

From: Self

Terry must come up with documentation on: (1) Purchase of 8 desks, 8 swivel chairs, 21 filing cabinets for Executive Wing—various dates, '35. Who besides Dutton bid on this? (2) Rejection of Kremer bid on carpet-cleaning contract. Why? It was low. (3) Why did it cost White House 27% more for heating Oct. '35–Jan. '36 than for same months last year? Weather colder? See specs, bids, contracts, etc.

"He was asking questions," said Layman. "I've found no evidence of any conclusions."

"These questions are appropriate ones for an auditor looking at the operations of a government office, are they not?" asked Mrs. Roosevelt.

"Yes, of course. But they are questions, let me emphasize. They do not draw conclusions."

"In the circumstances," said the First Lady, "the fact that he was asking such questions could be more important than the answers."

Stan Szczygiel arrived not long after.

"Yesterday afternoon I got through on the telephone to the United States District Attorney in New Orleans," he said. "I just got a telegram from him."

He handed the telegram to Mrs. Roosevelt. It read:

CAN CONFIRM THAT ONE THERESE LONGPRE AKA TERRY LONGPRE SERVED A TERM OF SIXTY DAYS AT THE PLAQUEMINES PARISH PRISON FARM IN 1930 STOP THE CHARGE WAS EMBEZZLEMENT OF PUBLIC FUNDS STOP SUBJECT HAS NO OTHER CRIMINAL RECORD AND RE-

TURNED TO STATE GOVERNMENT EMPLOYMENT IMMEDIATELY ON RE-
LEASE STOP SUBJECT IS KNOWN IN NEW ORLEANS AS HAVING BEEN
QUOTE INTIMATE PERSONAL FRIEND END QUOTE OF HUEY LONG STOP
TOLLER, USDA

"I think I should go over to the jail and have another little chat with Miss Rolland," the First Lady said. "In the meantime, I too have successfully completed a telephone call and have a line of inquiry you and Lieutenant Kennelly might want to pursue."

"And what is that, Ma'am?"

"Potassium cyanide is used to clean gold and silver objects. Find shops in Washington that use it for that purpose. Ask if any is missing. I am told that pawnshops as well as jewelers sometimes restore the luster of jewelry and silver serving pieces by immersing them in a bath of potassium cyanide. I shouldn't think there would be many such establishments in Washington."

Szczygiel smiled wryly. "I'm sure Ed Kennelly will be happy to put some men to work on that line of inquiry."

John Evans was the lawyer for Thérèse Rolland. He had taken her case at Mrs. Roosevelt's request, and on Saturday morning he came to the White House.

"I feel obliged to tell you, Mr. Evans," the First Lady said to him, "that we've learned that Mr. Duroc was working on an audit of Terry's operations here in the White House. We don't know that he had found anything wrong, but there is a file with notes in it that tell us he was looking into the way she handled bids and contracts."

"Motive . . ." Evans mused.

John Evans—inevitably called Jack—was one of the new

breed of lawyers attracted to Washington by the New Deal. A graduate of the law school of the University of Michigan, he had come to Washington as a clerk to Justice Benjamin Cardozo and had served two years with the justice; then, instead of heading off to practice law in New York, Boston, or Chicago, had decided that opportunity for a lucrative practice now existed in Washington. He had joined a small firm and had become, chiefly, a securities lawyer, a specialist in securing approval for stock issues from the new Securities and Exchange Commission. He had agreed, however, since the request came from the White House, to represent Thérèse Rolland.

Jack Evans was a diminutive, compact man, prematurely bald in his early thirties. He was usually somber and intent. People who liked him remarked his intelligence and sincerity. People who didn't thought he was pushy and self-important.

"I find myself in a somewhat anomalous position," said Mrs. Roosevelt. "I am working closely with the detectives investigating the case against Miss Rolland and am taken into their confidence. At the same time, I am trying to help her."

"I've had more cooperation from the police than I expected," said Evans. "I know that is because of your interest."

"Did she tell you she was sentenced to a term on a Louisiana prison farm, for misuse of state government funds?"

"My heavens, no," said Evans, genuinely surprised. "I'm sorry to say, she didn't."

"In 1930," said Mrs. Roosevelt. "Sixty days."

Evans shook his head. "That doesn't help. On the other

hand, that old conviction, for an entirely different kind of crime, has nothing to do with the charge against her now."

The First Lady shrugged. "That won't sound good to a jury, will it?"

"I think I can prevent a jury from hearing about it," said Evans.

Mrs. Roosevelt nodded. "Well . . . I plan to go over to the jail sometime today, to take some books and a basket of fruit to Miss Rolland. I believe I will ask her why she withheld from both of us the information that she was imprisoned in Louisiana."

Leaving her office, the First Lady took the elevator to the ground floor, then walked out through the colonnade and across to the West Wing. She found Sandra Wilson at work at her desk.

"I am glad to find you here, Sandra."

"Mr. Hopkins has been kind to me," said the plump little secretary. "I'm organizing Mr. Duroc's files, separating some personal things from official things, and boxing them up. Next week, I'll be working for a new boss."

Mrs. Roosevelt nodded. "Good. I am glad you will continue with us. I want to ask you a question, Sandra." Mrs. Roosevelt paused for a minute, for a moment distracted. Then she recovered her thought and asked, "When Mr. Duroc left the office, did he lock it?"

"No. Even when he went to lunch, he left it unlocked, in case I needed to go in and pick up something. He locked his desk. Also, the filing cabinets were usually locked. I could put stuff in his IN basket or take something from his OUT basket, but he kept all his confidential papers locked in the desk or files."

"Could someone have entered his office without your noticing?"

"Yes. I'm away from my desk now and then during the day. To the mail room. To the ladies' room. To lunch. Carrying papers to other offices."

"Very well. Thank you, Sandra. I'm glad Mr. Hopkins found another place for you. Feel welcome to call on me if any problem develops."

"It wasn't like this. It wasn't like this at all. Only just overnight, just one night, was I locked up in a cell."

Terry Rolland leaned against the bars, one arm shoved out between two bars and the fist clenched around one. She had just complained bitterly about how terrible it was to be in jail, and Mrs. Roosevelt had remarked that this wasn't the first time.

"Yes, it's true. I guess I should've told you I was sent to a prison farm in Louisiana. But it wasn't like *this*." She shook her head and smiled wanly. "You should've seen me, wearin' black-and-white stripes: convict's clothes, all loose, with the legs and sleeves rolled up 'cause they didn't have any small enough for me. Also a big, floppy straw hat. Barefoot. The work was hoein' the sugarcane fields, choppin' out the weeds. We only worked four hours a day, from six in the mornin' to ten—'cause it got too hot after that—but it was hard, sweaty work while we were at it. Afternoons, we did the kitchen work, sittin' in the shade, peelin' potatoes, snappin' beans, talkin'. There was never but two white women there while I was at the place. The two of us kep' apart and talked. She . . . Th' other woman was there for runnin' a still. But we were never locked up like this. We weren't kept in . . . *cages*. We slept in a sort of barracks."

"If you were a protégé of Governor Long, why didn't he see to it that you didn't have to serve a sentence?"

Terry grinned sourly and shook her head. "Mrs. Roosevelt, it was Huey that *put* me there! He wanted me there. Teach me a lesson. I'd got too uppity, was the way he put it. Too independent was what he meant. He sent me to the Plaquemines Parish prison farm to give me a taste of what he could do to a person who got outa line. It was nothin', compared to what he did to people who *really* got outa line. There are *graves* in Louisiana occupied by people that turned against Huey Long. And if you think Dr. Weise was the one that killed him, you were born yesterday!"

"Are you telling me you were not guilty of the charges against you?"

Terry shrugged. "I did what I was told to do. The Long machine has its ways. In Louisiana, you don't sell a ton of bricks or concrete to a parish or to the state without you pay a percentage to the machine. You don't *teach school* in Louisiana without you hand over a percentage of your wages." She shrugged again. "So different from any other state? What's the payback from a guy who puts a roof on a New York school? Wasn't there somethin' in the paper about that, not so long ago?"

"What about your White House purchasing contracts?" asked Mrs. Roosevelt.

Terry shook her head emphatically. "I swear to you, as God is my witness, that I never played any kind of game with White House contracts. Hell . . . Mrs. Roosevelt. . . . I wouldn't have known how! Nobody ever told me to shake down sellers. If I took fifteen percent of a federal contract, who'd I pay it over to?"

"You were being audited by Mr. Duroc."

"Right. But he didn't find anything."

"Maybe he was interrupted before he could find anything," said Mrs. Roosevelt.

Terry swung around and gripped another bar with her right hand. "Oh . . . The motive . . ." she whispered. "You closin' the trap on me?"

"No. I want to believe you are innocent. But you have not been candid, Terry."

Terry blew out a loud, fluttering breath. "I'm confused," she said quietly. "You're outside, doing things, seeing things, talkin' to people." She glanced around the cell. "Me . . . This is it. I don't hardly know what day it is. What difference, anyway? It's like I'm in a different little world."

"Mr. Evans came to see me this morning," said Mrs. Roosevelt. "You must be completely candid with him, Terry. Even if you can't be with me, you must be with him. I won't betray a confidence of yours, but he *can't*. He's your lawyer."

Terry had closed her eyes. "Miz Roosevelt," she said. "My daddy's comin' up on a train to see me. Is there *any way* you can arrange for him to see me somewheres outside this jail, dressed in ordinary clothes? He saw me at the prison farm, and that nearly killed him. It would of, but he knew why I was there. I mean, he knew it was political. This . . . This is somethin' else agin. It'll just kill him."

"I'll speak to Lieutenant Kennelly. I'm sure something can be arranged."

"I'll be grateful."

When Mrs. Roosevelt returned to the White House after her Saturday-afternoon visit to the jail, she found a telephone note in her office saying Stan Szczygiel wanted to talk to her. She didn't have to telephone the Secret Service office to say she was in. He knew she was in; the gate reported her return; and he arrived shortly on the second floor.

"I thought you would want to know that Father Claude Duroc has arrived in Washington to claim his brother's body."

"A priest?"

Szczygiel nodded.

"Oh dear. I feel we should do something. I mean, we should somehow extend our condolences."

"He is still at police headquarters—or was when I last spoke with Kennelly, ten minutes ago."

"Telephone Lieutenant Kennelly, will you please, and ask him to bring Father Claude here—that is, if he wants to come."

At six-thirty, when the President, Missy, and Harry Hopkins were having their cocktails in the second-floor hall, the First Lady received Father Claude Duroc in the Green Room.

The priest turned out to be a younger brother of the murder victim. He was the parish priest of a parish in Baton Rouge. Dressed in a shiny black suit, with pectoral cross and Roman collar, he was no more than five feet four, yet a man with some command in his presence, owing probably to the intensity of his personality. He had the air not of a man in mourning, just of a man doing a grim duty.

Mrs. Roosevelt expressed her sympathy, and the priest said—

"I will give that word to my family, who will be grateful. I am afraid, to be altogether frank about it, that the family had some fear that Paul would come to a tragic end."

The comment generated an awkward moment. Stan Szczygiel and Ed Kennelly exchanged glances, and the First Lady turned her attention to the trays brought up from the kitchen.

"We've some sandwiches, Father," she said. "Coffee and tea. Or, if you would like something a bit more fortifying, we have sherry, whiskey, and gin."

"Scotch," said the priest. "Yes, I will have a tot of that." Szczygiel rose to pour. "Soda?" he asked. "Water?"

"Neat," said Father Claude.

"Ahh . . . You are a large family?" asked Mrs. Roosevelt, trying to make talk that would relieve the awkwardness of the moment.

The priest held his glass up before him, waiting for others to be served before he drank. "Yes," he said. "Five sons, two daughters. My parents are both alive. My eldest brother is also in holy orders."

"Your parents must be proud of that," said Szczygiel.

Father Claude smiled faintly. "They like their grandchildren," he said. "Their two sons in orders produced none, and . . . neither did Paul."

Mrs. Roosevelt accepted a sherry from Szczygiel. All had glasses, and she lifted hers and said, "We are pleased to meet you, Father, and only wish it could be in happier circumstances."

"I hope it does not prove true," the priest said solemnly, "that Thérèse Rolland killed my brother. I was chaplain at the Plaquemines Parish prison farm when she served her time there. I cannot believe she could commit murder. She was a troubled young woman. I cannot say more. But I find it distinctly difficult to think she could be capable of intentionally taking the life of another human being."

"An interesting coincidence," said Kennelly.

"No," said Father Claude. "I introduced her to Paul, in the hope that he could help her. In turn, she introduced Paul to Governor Long—with results I could not have anticipated."

"Will you expand on that thought, Father?" asked Mrs. Roosevelt.

The priest had emptied his glass at a gulp and now handed it to Szczygiel for another splash of Scotch. "My parents had hoped Paul would enter the Church—rather than that I should, actually. We had to understand, though, that poverty, chastity, and obedience were not for Paul." He smiled again, this time more broadly. "I am not sure which of the three offended him most."

Kennelly laughed.

"Paul enjoyed life—without much thought, I am afraid, for the life to come. He was reckless. He actually established a meretricious relationship with a young woman on whom . . . How shall I say it? With a young woman on whom Governor Long had placed his brand. *That* was reckless."

"What young woman?" asked Mrs. Roosevelt.

"Why, Thérèse Rolland, of course. Didn't you know?"

The First Lady was having dinner with her close friend Lorena Hickock. "Hick" had been a journalist covering Franklin D. Roosevelt from 1928 on. She and Mrs. Roosevelt had become close friends, and when the Roosevelts moved into the White House, it was arranged for Hick to have a government job. When it became apparent that Louis Howe would never recover and would never return from his hospital room to the room he had occupied on the third floor of the White House, the First Lady arranged for Hick to have that room. The two women would have liked to see each other daily, but that had proved impossible. They had not been together alone yet this week, so the dinner had been arranged. They would have it in the First Lady's bedroom, from trays, just as the President was having his two rooms away, with Missy.

Hick was a short, fat woman with a pug face. (Someone once said of her that she looked like she should be smoking the stub of a cigar.) She was entirely sympathetic to Elea-nor Roosevelt, and was probably her closest personal friend in 1936. Hick had seen and understood the dismay on Mrs. Roosevelt's face as she listened to the election returns in 1932 and realized she was to be First Lady. When everyone else was offering happy congratulations, only Lorena Hick-ock was sensitive to see that her friend was frightened, took her hand, and expressed concern.

Dressed in nightgowns, the two friends ate from their trays and listened to a concert on the radio—a recital by the soprano Jessica Dragonette. After that they would lis-ten to a broadcast concert by the Chicago Symphony.

Mrs. Roosevelt was relaxed. She could relax with Hick. The fat little woman reached for the tall woman's hand and squeezed it. Mrs. Roosevelt clasped Hick's hand. She closed her eyes and smiled serenely.

Because it was very difficult for the President to attend a theater or go to a movie house, Hollywood producers sent films to the White House—16-mm versions of their most popular pictures—and the Bell & Howell Company had provided a 16-mm sound projector. Missy LeHand had learned to operate the somewhat complicated projector, and occasionally she and the President enjoyed a film in his bedroom.

After the evening cocktail hour, the President's valet, Arthur Prettyman, helped him with his bath and helped him into bed, where he sat in his pajamas, propped up against a heap of pillows. Tonight, Arthur set up the screen against the east wall of the room and the projector on a table near the west wall.

Missy arrived shortly after the valet left and before the dinner trays were delivered. She was dressed in a blue nightgown and a white peignoir.

"What are we seeing tonight?" she asked.

"Something I'm going to love," said the President with a grin. *"Mutiny on the Bounty*! With Charles Laughton as Captain Bligh and Clark Gable as Fletcher Christian."

"Good."

The film was a year old, and both of them had read newspaper accounts of it. Both had, of course, read the book. The President, who loved ships and the sea and had been an active sailor before he lost the use of his legs, had been looking forward to *Mutiny on the Bounty.*

"We have to eat first," said the President. "Have you seen the cables?"

Missy shook her head. The President pointed at a small leather-bound folder on his night table and gestured that she should open it and read the telegrams inside.

At dawn that morning, German troops had crossed the Rhine bridges and occupied the Rhineland. The Rhineland was part of Germany, but the German government was bound by treaty not to station armed forces there. The treaty that bound them was not just the Treaty of Versailles, which Hitler condemned as having been forced on

Germany in 1919, but the later Locarno Treaty, which Germany had entered into entirely voluntarily in 1925.

France was entitled to take military action to prevent Germany from militarizing the Rhineland. Britain was tied by treaty to support France if France took such action. For a few morning hours, the President had wondered if an armed clash was not about to develop along the German-French frontier.

But it didn't. The French did not move.

The first wire in the folder was from the German foreign minister, Baron Konstantin von Neurath. It read—

FRANCE'S NEGATION OF THE TREATY OF LOCARNO BY ENTERING INTO AN ALLIANCE WITH THE SOVIET UNION RELEASES GERMANY FROM ALL OBLIGATION UNDER THAT TREATY STOP GERMANY'S ACTION TODAY IN RE-STATIONING MILITARY FORCES IN THE RHINELAND CONSTITUTES NOTHING MORE THAN RE-OCCUPATION OF GERMAN TERRITORY BY GERMAN FORCES STOP I AM AUTHORIZED BY THE FUEHRER TO ASSURE YOU THAT THIS MOVEMENT OF A TOKEN FORCE IS FOR THE SOLE PURPOSE OF REASSERTING GERMAN SOVEREIGNTY OVER TERRITORY UNIVERSALLY RECOGNIZED AS GERMAN STOP IT HAS NO OTHER DIPLO-MATIC OR MILITARY SIGNIFICANCE STOP

VON NEURATH

The second telegram in the folder was from Anthony Eden, British foreign secretary. It read—

HIS MAJESTY'S GOVERNMENT ARE SATISFIED WE HAVE NO REASON TO SUPPOSE THAT GERMANY'S PRESENT ACTION THREATENS HOSTILITIES STOP

EDEN, FOREIGN SECRETARY

"Apparently this morning's alarm was premature," said the President.

"I'll be interested to hear what that fellow Churchill has to say," Missy remarked.

"We know what he'll have to say. Alarum, alarum. But Chancellor Hitler seems to think he has the right to tear up treaties whenever he decides somebody else has violated them. His rationalization is not very convincing."

As Missy returned the folder to his night table, she caressed the President's forehead and cheek. "Effdee," she said, "I thought we were going to concentrate on a movie this evening."

They were interrupted by a discreet knock on the door. A maid from the kitchen wheeled in a cart bearing the dinner trays, coffee, and a bottle of brandy.

Missy took care of fixing the President's tray before him on his lap. Then she shed her peignoir and sat down on the bed beside him, with her own tray.

V

On Sunday the President sometimes went to church. This Sunday he did not, nor did Mrs. Roosevelt. Instead she went horseback riding in Rock Creek Park. Lenora Hickock did not ride. The First Lady's friend Eleanor Morgenthau did, and they rode together for more than an hour. Two southern newspapers would take note of it editorially the next day, comparing her going riding on Sunday to the sinful practice of growing numbers of businessmen who played golf on Sunday morning.

A South Carolina paper used the incident as an argument for its ongoing campaign to keep golf courses closed on Sundays, at least until noon: "What an example La Eleanor sets for our young people! If the wife of the President of the United States chooses to amuse herself horseback riding on Sunday morning, neglecting divine services, what can we expect of Miss Wilkinson, daughter of the president of our Chamber of Commerce, who on Sunday morning regularly entertains her young crowd at what they call 'brunch'?"

Ed Kennelly, who ordinarily worked a six-day week, took off enough time that Sunday morning to attend an early mass, then checked in at headquarters. Faced with an unsolved murder that had occurred in the Executive Wing of the White House, he did not feel free to take the day off.

On impulse, he walked back into the jail. He found Terry Rolland lying on her cot, looking about half asleep but with pencil in hand and a big crossword puzzle in front of her.

"How ya doin'?" he asked her.

She sat up and put down her puzzle. "I'd rather be dead than—"

"That's what Duroc is. Dead."

"I didn't kill him," she said dully. "Does that make any difference?"

"His brother came to pick up his body."

"I know. He came to see me. He heard my confession."

"That's more than I've heard," said Kennelly dryly.

"That's what you'd like, wouldn't you? A confession. Whether I did it or not."

Kennelly lit a Lucky. "Not if you didn't do it, Terry. Not if you didn't do it. Your father is in town. I'm gonna let you have lunch with him, in a restaurant. Mrs. Roosevelt asked me to do something like that. Smoke?"

She shook her head. "I don't smoke."

"Really? Come to think of it, you haven't asked for butts. You haven't been smokin' in here."

"I don't smoke," she said.

Back in his office he thought about that for a minute. Duroc had smoked Spuds. The ashtrays in his house had been filled with the butts of Spuds and Luckies. He'd been inclined to suspect Terry had been spending a lot of time in

Duroc's house and bedroom. But maybe not. And if not Terry, who?

Sitting at his desk a few minutes later, Kennelly looked over a brief report that had been handed to him yesterday. A dozen or so telephone numbers had been written on the cover and early pages of the telephone directory in Terry's room. An officer had been assigned to identify those numbers, and this was his report.

He had identified all the numbers, using a reverse telephone directory. All were listed numbers. The telephone company confirmed that all were current. One of the numbers was Duroc's. None of the remaining names meant anything to Kennelly. He sent the report back to the man who had made it, ordering him to find out who all the listed people were.

At eleven-thirty a matron took Terry from her cell to a shower, where she watched her bathe; she then handed Terry the clothes she had been wearing when she was arrested. Terry dressed and put on a little makeup. She protested when the matron handcuffed her, but the matron promised to take the cuffs off before her father saw her. The matron went with her in a police car to the Dixon Hotel. A detective came out to confirm that Horace Rolland was waiting in the restaurant. The matron took off the handcuffs and led Terry into the hotel. She left her at the door into the restaurant.

"We have the exits covered," she told Terry.

Her father stood when he saw her. He was a short, wizened man, a bit hunched. His iron-gray hair was smoothed and held down by hair tonic. His thin, deeply wrinkled face was a rigid mask of gravity and decorum, outrage and scorn.

"Ah *understood*," he said to her, "that you are in *jail*. How is it you can come here?"

"They let me come to have lunch with you."

He shook his head as they sat down. "You can go out when you want?"

"Well . . . I'm in custody, Daddy."

"You're in jail, is what you are." He sniffed. "They say you killed Paul Duroc."

"I didn't do it."

"No, course not. You have a lawyer?"

"Yes. Mrs. Roosevelt got me a lawyer. He's supposed to be a very good one."

"You figure the *Longs* have anything to do with this?"

Terry shook her head.

"I understand I can't post bail for you. You're being held on a murder charge. If you're convicted—" He shook his head. "You'll likely be hung. Or electrocuted."

"I'm not a murderer, Daddy," she said tearfully.

"No, I don't think you are. You're a whoah, is what you are."

She sobbed. "I'm not that either, Daddy."

He shrugged and turned his eyes to the menu. "Why not? Your mother was."

"*Daddy . . .*"

"She was. In Storyville. For three years. But you were a whoah to Huey Long for more years than that. Your mother had the good sense to save her money and get out of that life. You never did."

"Do you hate me, Daddy?"

"No—"

He stopped because their waitress had come to the table. He ordered pan-fried steak and grits. Terry said she'd have the same. When the waitress was gone, Horace Rolland continued—

"No, I don't hate you, Thérèse. You are what you are, and I can't blame you for being it. I don't want you to hang. On the other hand, I think a few years in jail would probably be good for you. Come out, you'll be too old to be a whoah."

When the matron handcuffed her again, in the lobby of the hotel, Terry glanced back and saw that her father had come out of the restaurant and was watching. She dropped her chin to her chest and wept quietly as the matron led her to the car.

Father Claude Duroc was grateful to Ed Kennelly. He knew the police detective had gone out of his way to be helpful in the unhappy process of claiming a body from a morgue and arranging for it to be shipped home. Kennelly had even taken the priest to the little house Paul Duroc had rented and allowed him to select clothes to be put on the body, so it wouldn't be put in its coffin naked. So grateful was Father Claude that he didn't refuse Kennelly's invitation to have dinner with him, although he expected he would be subjected to intense interrogation.

Kennelly took the priest to Harvey's, a fine and expensive restaurant. They sat down at a table not far from J. Edgar Hoover and his boyfriend Clyde Tolson, who dined there almost every night and never paid a check.

"I will not suggest you violate the secrecy of the confessional, Father," said Kennelly, "but I will ask you to understand that I am investigating a murder."

"The victim was my brother," said Father Claude somberly.

"You said you hoped it would turn out that Thérèse Rolland is not the killer. May I ask why you feel that way?"

"At the prison farm in Plaquemines Parish I developed a strong sympathy for Terry Rolland. She was a victim. I am sure she was a victim. When she came there, she was terrified, humiliated . . . just shattered."

"She talks about being ashamed to face her father."

"Ed . . . Terry's father is a professional gambler, sometime pimp, one-time bootlegger, and confidence man. Her mother was a prostitute in a bawdy house in Storyville. Terry is their only child, and they were determined she'd become something better than they ever were. Interesting, isn't it? Parents with that background still wanting their daughter to be something better. I suppose she figures she's failed them. Terry's father himself served two short terms, one on a county farm, one in the state penitentiary. Even so, he holds himself high. So does her mother, now."

"Do they have money?" Kennelly asked skeptically.

Father Claude grinned. "How does the song go? I probably don't have this exactly right, but. He lowered his voice, leaned across the table, and sang—

> *My mother makes beer in the bathtub,*
> *My father sells bootlegger gin,*
> *My sister makes love for a living,*
> *My God, how the money rolls in!*
> *It ro-olls in! It ro-olls in!*
> *My God, how the money rolls in!*

The smiling priest shrugged. "There's money in that kind of life, on the edge of society, on the wrong side of the law." Kennelly laughed.

"They had Terry educated by nuns, in a private school where nobody—especially the nuns—had an inkling of who she was. Then they sent her to Tulane University. She graduated with a degree in economics in 1926. I don't know if she met Huey Long while she was a student or if she met him after she went to work for the Railroad Commission. He was a railroad commissioner, so she may have met him after she went to work for the commission. Anyway, it wasn't very long before she and Huey were . . . Well, you know what I mean. He said once he'd never had a redhead. He had one now."

"Then what was she doing on a prison farm?"

"Tried to end the relationship with Huey, according to her. He wanted to make her understand that somebody committed to Huey Long stayed with Huey long until *he* decided it was to end."

"He could get away with that?"

Father Claude smiled. "Huey Long could get away with anything. You think he was governor? Oh, no. He was *king.* The Kingfish. Why . . . One time a henchman of his was before a judge for sentencing. He'd beaten somebody up, for Huey. A political opponent. The judge sentenced the fellow to sixty days in jail. The fellow laughed and handed the judge a pardon signed by Governor Long. Huey'd pardoned him before he was sentenced!"

"If a president abused the pardon power like that, he'd be impeached," said Kennelly.

"Don't bet on it," said the priest dryly.

"Why in the world did you introduce her to your brother?" Kennelly asked.

"I thought I could help her. Paul was a strong personality. He was attractive to women and attracted by them. I naively thought he might be able to rescue her from the clutches of Huey Long."

"How was he gonna do that, his influence being like you've described?"

"Paul had an offer from a California university. He was a well-regarded professor, and the California school had offered him a full professorship and more money. I suggested he take Terry with him to California. Huey's writ didn't run across the state line." The priest shook his head. "Instead, she introduced Paul to Huey. The governor used his charm on Paul, and the first thing I know, Paul was another Long henchman. He got Paul elected to the legislature. Then he brought him up to Washington. Also Terry."

"Would anyone in the Long machine have had reason to kill him?" Kennelly asked.

Father Claude sighed. "Who can say? I can tell you this: My brother loved money and all the things it can buy. I am certain his association with the Long machine corrupted him. Other members of the family may come to Washington. My father, for one, is certain Paul had money. I mean, a great deal of money. Hidden."

"I can tell you how much he had in his checking account," said Kennelly. "Just a little over a hundred dollars."

"I'll bet there's more money somewhere. Paul wouldn't have lived in Washington with no more than a hundred dollars in his bank account."

Their waiter appeared at last, and they gave him an order for drinks. The priest lit his pipe.

"Father . . ." said Kennelly. "We found the key to a safe-deposit box. But we don't know the box number or the name of the bank. Do you have any idea?"

Father Claude shook his head.

"Where would this money have come from?" Kennelly asked. "What would he have done to get it?"

"I am not wise in the ways of machine politicians," said the priest.

"He seems to have been living with a woman. Do you have any idea who that could have been?"

"Thérèse Rolland, I should imagine."

Kennelly shook his head. "I don't think so. I'm not sure, but I don't think so. Any other ideas?"

"He made many new friends since he moved to Washington."

Kennelly arrived at the White House a little after four. Mrs. Roosevelt was meeting with a committee of Midwestern Democrats, most of them the wives of Democratic candidates for Congress. He waited half an hour before she was available.

They sat down together in the Red Room, where the committee had met. There was still hot coffee and clean cups, and she poured coffee for both of them.

"I'm developing a suspicion," said Kennelly. "I still think Terry Rolland killed Paul Duroc, but I'm starting to get an idea of the motive."

"I am interested," said the First Lady.

"Both of them worked for Huey Long," said Kennelly. "In the first place, how did two Long people get jobs in the White House?"

Mrs. Roosevelt smiled. "Practical politics, Lieutenant,"

she said. "Until Senator Long decided to run for president himself, he was a supporter of my husband's programs. He was a vote in the Senate and sometimes a persuasive voice. When he asked for a job for someone, usually he got it. Not always. Usually."

"Who did you figure those people really worked for?" asked Kennelly. "The President or Huey Long?"

The First Lady smiled again. "Both," she said. "We had to understand that. Both. On the other hand, Mr. Duroc seems to have been an effective auditor who turned up some improprieties in the spending of government money. Unless his pending audit of Miss Rolland turns up irregularities, she did an effective job, too."

"But they were working for Huey at the same time," said Kennelly. "Right?"

"The cliché, Lieutenant, is that they knew which side their bread was buttered on. I have no doubt they knew."

"Let me tell you why I asked to see you on Sunday afternoon," said Kennelly. "I figure the key to the case may be in exactly what each of them did for Huey Long. I . . . I know what Terry did—at least part of what she did. She slept with him. I dictated a memo this afternoon on Terry's life and times. I'll have a copy delivered to you as soon as possible."

"Give me the worst, Lieutenant," said Mrs. Roosevelt. "Unless I misunderstand you, you are suggesting I make some calls to people in Louisiana to see what I can find out. I can't do that in the dark."

Kennelly returned his empty coffee cup to the table. "Her father is a confidence man and professional gambler who has himself served time. Her mother was a Storyville prostitute. Terry herself is a university graduate but she became a . . . mistress to Huey Long."

"I shall see what more I can learn," said Mrs. Roosevelt.

Sunday though it was, the President met late in the day with a man he trusted.

John Lowell Endicott had been the President's friend for many years, since they met at Harvard. They had not been in the same class, but they were there together, and their friendship had endured, firm and fast, over the years.

Endicott was a Bostonian. Known as "Blackjack" for his fondness for that game, he was also known as a playboy. And that he was: pilot, yachtsman, polo player, master at bridge . . . He was, on the other hand, a shrewd investor and a careful manager of his inheritance. He was no shallow bon vivant but an intelligent, active man of the world. Tall, handsome, dark, wearing always a black pencil mustache, he was, in many ways, what Frank Roosevelt wished he could be.

"Your intelligence sources must be much better than mine," he said to the President.

Appreciating the unhappy state of the White House wine cellars, he had brought with him two bottles of Chateau Lafitte, which he and the President had allowed to breathe for a time and were now sharing, with the Stilton cheese and paté de foie gras Blackjack had also brought.

"I cannot be sure," said the President. "What do you hear?"

"I am not sure how much confidence you place in Winston Churchill," said Blackjack Endicott. "For myself, I suspect he knows more than British and American intelligence agencies combined. People talk to him. People tell him the unhappy truth."

"You spoke with him?"

Blackjack nodded. "Actually, he spoke with me. He called me and asked me to give you some information."

"In confidence."

"In confidence."

"Okay, Jack. Let's hear it."

Blackjack Endicott blew a sigh. "The Germans moved *three battalions* across the Rhine yesterday. Three . . . battalions. The French have *one hundred divisions* facing the German frontier. If the French move, they can sweep those German battalions back across the Rhine in a few hours. But they won't."

"They won't?"

Blackjack shook his head. "They won't. They've lost their nerve. They are not the French nation we knew in 1917 and 1918. They won't, and because they won't, they will lose more than they can guess."

"Churchill?"

"Churchill," said Blackjack, nodding.

"So what does Mr. Churchill think?"

"I agree with what he thinks. He thinks the Germans will fortify the Rhineland. They won't have to alarm the French by moving many divisions into the area. They will use civilian labor to build what they will call a West Wall. If the French move tomorrow, a single French division can drive Hitler's three battalions back across the Rhine. If they delay six months, they will need five divisions. A year from now they will need twenty. Two years from now, or four, their entire hundred divisions will not be enough. Hitler's remilitarization of the Rhineland is the opening gun of another world war!"

"Surely . . ."

"You don't want to believe it," said Blackjack. "I don't want to believe it. And, for damned sure, the Congress doesn't want to believe it. But there you have it. I am sure Winston Churchill is right."

"My hands are tied, Jack. You know that. I can hardly persuade the Congress to maintain what military and naval strength we have, much less appropriate money for more."

Blackjack Endicott shrugged. "What can I do for you, Frank?"

"You've done much for me over the years," said the President. "Not the least of which is to bring me something marvelous to eat, to relieve the tuna-sandwich diet my wife thinks is good enough for me."

Blackjack laughed. "God, I will never forget what she told a press conference in 1932: that she could serve you scrambled eggs every night for a week and you wouldn't notice the difference!"

"*She* wouldn't notice the difference," said the President. "My only reservation about Abraham Lincoln, as to whether he was a great man or not, is the quotation from him that he never cared what he ate. Ahh . . . Entertain me, my dear friend. As we share this excellent wine, tell me about your triumphs at table, on the playing field, at sea, and . . . and in the boudoir!"

VI

On Monday, Mrs. Roosevelt began her day by dictating her newspaper column to her secretary. She chose as her subject the remilitarization of the Rhineland.

There can be no question but that the Treaty of Versailles was in some respects unfair, which the Germans resent. France, on the other hand, cannot forget that twice in the past sixty-five years it has been invaded by Germany. If the Germans will take into account the justified apprehensions of the French and the French will take into account the justified resentment of the Germans, a peaceful settlement of the two nations' differences can be arrived at. Such a settlement must be fair to both nations. Surely the French and German statesmen can find a basis for an equitable adjustment.

Her column was called "My Day," and it appeared in more than sixty newspapers, with circulation of more than four million. She had begun writing it about three months ago. No matter how busy her schedule, she never missed a deadline. She found that she enjoyed writing it.

Her secret ambition was to write a novel or a play.

When she finished the column, she placed a telephone call to the Superintendent of the Senate Press Galley and asked him to tell Robert Packard, correspondent for the *Shreveport Times*, that she would appreciate his calling her. She had met Packard a few weeks ago at a dinner, and they had chatted for a few minutes. She realized he was the only Louisiana newspaperman she knew.

Packard called a few minutes later.

"I appreciate your calling me so promptly," she said to him. "I hope you won't mind if I ask you a few questions."

"Not at all, Ma'am," said Packard. He spoke with a deep southern accent, peppered with Cajun expressions, including the Cajun predilection for reversing the structure of a phrase or sentence. "I'm glad to hear from you. How y'are?"

"Very well, thank you. And you?"

"Fine as frog's hair. What can I do for you?"

"I am sure you know that one of your fellow Louisianans was murdered here last week and another is in jail and charged with the crime."

"I know. My editor has called me six or five times, wantin' information about it."

"Mr. Packard, what can you tell me about Mr. Duroc and Miss Rolland?"

"In confidence?"

"Yes. Confidentially."

"Miz Roosevelt, I expect you know what a bag man is."

"I believe I do. He is a person who collects money for a candidate or a party."

"Exactly. Well . . . Paul Duroc was the Washin'ton bag man for Huey Long. Huey was puttin' together a war chest for a campaign for president this year. What he had to rely on mostly was dimes and nickels from all over the country: like the fifty-dollah, fo'ty-dollah contribution. But a few big lobbyists were hedgin' their bets. Huey was musclin' 'em for money, and a few of them were coughin' up. Paul Duroc was the unofficial and confidential treasurer."

"How much money are we talking about, do you know?"

"No. I've got no idea. But I can guess. We're talkin', mos' likely, about a hund'ed thousand, fifty thousand dollahs. Huey was just gettin' started."

"Where is that money now? Do you know?"

"That's the big question, Miz Roosevelt. I can think of three places where it might be. First, Paul paid it over to the Long machine in Loosy-ana. Second, some of them lobbyists demanded it back, since Huey's dead and not gonna run, and Paul paid it back, or some of it. Three, he kep' it. If he kep' it, *there'd* be reason somebody'd kill him, wouldn't it?"

"What do you think Miss Rolland had to do with this? If anything?"

"She was one of Huey's girls."

"He arranged to have her imprisoned," said Mrs. Roosevelt.

"I've heard that story. Fact, I've seen the story. We didn't run it, our paper. We didn't run it. Now, this next is most confidential. Huey did things like that. I don't know what she did to get herself in his bad graces, but she was lucky, if it was anythin' much, to get off with jus' some time on the county farm. 'Course, they wuz reconciled. After all, he brought her to Washin'ton. Carryin' coals to Newcastle is how he put it."

"Here in Washington, she was—"

"I cain't put the matter delicate, Ma'am. He was never seen with her in public. But in private . . . Private parties, she was *his*. He liked her. Liked to show her off. He had more beautiful girls, I s'pose, but none more *strikin'*."

"Was there any truth to the charges on which she was sent to the prison farm?"

"Could've been. That would've tickled Huey: to send her away for doin' exactly what he'd appointed her to do."

"What was her function here in Washington, apart from being the senator's plaything?"

"I never heard she was here for any other reason—that is, any reason of Huey's. Course, he put her on the federal payroll, so's he wouldn't have t' pay her expenses."

"Can you suggest any reason why she would want to kill Paul Duroc?"

"Dumb thing for her to do, if she did it."

Stan Szczygiel and Ed Kennelly arrived for a meeting with the First Lady.

"Fingerprints," said Kennelly. "J. Edgar Hoover to the contrary notwithstanding, we hardly ever solve a crime by finding fingerprints. No crooks are stupid enough to leave fingerprints around anymore."

"Which means . . . ?"

"The boys found two sets of fingerprints in Duroc's house. His, of course. But the others—" He shrugged. "Lots of nice clean prints, but those prints aren't on file anywhere."

"All over the cosmetics bottles," said Szczygiel. "And all over the house. The prints of somebody who was never arrested, never fingerprinted."

"I should surmise," said Mrs. Roosevelt, "that would include a substantial majority of the people of the United States."

"Right," said Kennelly. "You can get fingerprinted two ways in this country: one, get arrested; or, two, give your fingerprints in front of a newsreel camera with a beaming John Edgar Hoover looking on. His campaign to get the whole country voluntarily fingerprinted has been a bust."

"I should be reluctant to give my fingerprints," said Mrs. Roosevelt with a wide smile. "After all, I might someday wish to commit a crime."

Kennelly chuckled. "Wear gloves, Ma'am," he said. "If you want to commit a crime, wear gloves."

"So that line of inquiry leads us to nothing."

"Not necessarily," said Szczygiel. "If we can identify a woman we think might have lived with Duroc, we can match her prints to the ones found in the house."

"I had wondered if the woman in Mr. Duroc's house might not be Miss Rolland," said the First Lady.

"Not her fingerprints," said Kennelly. "Anyway, she doesn't smoke, and the woman in Duroc's house smoked Lucky Strikes."

"Well . . . Are you checking the jewelers, Lieutenant? I mean, are you looking for ones who clean gold and silver with potassium cyanide?"

"I've got somebody working on that," said Kennelly.

At noon Mrs. Roosevelt kept an appointment to visit an automobile show at the Armory. It would be opened the next day by the President, and after that large crowds were expected. The sponsors of the show had invited selected people for a box lunch and preview. They hoped to take photographs of the guests with the cars, before the crowds came.

An appearance at the show was something of an obligation for the First Lady. The automobile manufacturers and dealers had promoted the show in an effort to whet the public's appetite for new cars. That was not just business, their representative had argued to Mrs. Roosevelt when he brought her the invitation; it was a contribution to economic recovery. A widely circulated poster seen everywhere in those years showed a factory worker, lunch box in hand, arriving on his front porch and showing his happy wife his paycheck. The poster said—

WHEN YOU BUY AN AUTOMOBILE
YOU GIVE **3 MONTHS WORK** TO SOMEONE
Which Allows Him to Buy
OTHER PRODUCTS
Buy a Car Now—Help Bring Back Prosperity

As she had expected, the First Lady was met at the door, not only by a delegation of men anxious to lead her to their particular cars but also by a dozen press photographers carrying their big cameras and setting off their blinding flashbulbs.

Smiling dutifully, she allowed herself to be led in turn to an Auburn Straight 8, then to a LaSalle coupé, then to a long, dark-blue Packard. At each car someone opened the doors, sometimes lifted the doors of the hood, and pointed out features of the car to her. She mimed intense interest while flashbulbs popped.

She was led to a table, where a box lunch waited for her. She sat down, and a man from the Ford Motor Company took the seat to her right. He spoke urgently about the V-12 Lincoln Zephyr that she hadn't seen yet. Only after three or four minutes did she have a moment to turn and see who was at her left.

"Good effternoon, Mrs. . . . . Roosevelt."

It was Bela Lugosi, and if he had been wearing evening clothes instead of a gray three-piece suit he would have been Count Dracula. He needed but little makeup for the role. She realized too that the Dracula accent was only the Hungarian actor's natural voice.

"Oh, I am glad to meet you, Mr. Lugosi."

"The pleasure and honor . . . are mine," he said.

"Are you being photographed with automobiles?" she asked.

"Yes. Dey would of course rather photograph me with a hearsss," he said. He laughed.

Mrs. Roosevelt laughed, too. "I suppose so," she said. "You are so identified."

He nodded. "In the National Theater in Budapest, I was a *leading* man, the romantic lead, not a monstair."

"You are a skilled actor, Mr. Lugosi."

"Thank . . . you. My chief preoccupation today is to interest Americans in European-style football, what you call socc-air. I sponsair a league of players in California. They compete for the Bela Lugosi Trophy. I am hoping one of these automobile companies will join in sponsairing the league."

"I wish you luck," she said as a man from General Motors competed for her attention.

"We would like to show you an experimental car we have here, Mrs. Roosevelt," the man said. "And if you have time after the show closes, we'd like to bring the car to the White House and let you drive it."

"Experimental?" she asked. She had not had time even to open her box lunch. "What sort of experiment?"

"A car that shifts its own gears," the man said happily. "All you need do is press the accelerator, and the car selects the appropriate gear and shifts into it automatically."

"The Model T did that," she said.

"Ah, but not like this. The Model T had three pedals you had to manipulate, plus the throttle, spark, and brake. In this car there will be only two pedals on the floor: accelerator and brake. It will shift up and down, all very smoothly."

"That will make driving much easier," she said. "I think of my husband, driving his car about on the estate at Hyde Park. It would be easier for him, certainly."

They were interrupted by a commotion some distance away. Photographers gathered around a young woman sitting on the fender of a Duesenberg.

Mrs. Roosevelt recognized her. She was the Hollywood actress Jean Harlow, she of the platinum-blond hair, the eyebrows plucked to fine lines, she who was said to press ice cubes to her breasts before a movie shot to make her nipples stand up and show through her clothes. She had drawn her feet up on the fender of the Duesenberg, and the photographers were clamoring for her to allow her skirt to fall back and show her legs.

"I suspect," the First Lady said with a mock-ingenuous smile, "the newspapers will carry more pictures of that Duesenberg than of your experimental car."

The man from General Motors scowled, just as Jean Harlow let her skirt fall back halfway between her knees and hips, showing sleek legs and dark silk stockings. A score of flashbulbs made a blinding glare.

The car that most interested Mrs. Roosevelt was one that was being somewhat deferentially shown. The man showing it explained that it would not be offered on the market until 1937. Called a Cord, it was driven by a Lycoming V-8 engine that would apply power through the front wheels. The headlights were hidden inside the front fenders, behind doors that would open when the lights were switched on. The grille circled the entire engine compartment, all the way back to the doors. It was a convertible. Standing beside it, Mrs. Roosevelt was aware that its top stood no more than five feet above the floor. A person would have to bend down to get in it. That was important to road stability, the man said, since the Cord promised a top speed of more than one hundred miles an hour.

"It's the car of the future, Mrs. Roosevelt," said the man from the company.

She nodded, but she said quietly, "First we shall have to build roads on which automobiles can travel a hundred miles an hour."

As she left the Armory, Mrs. Roosevelt found Senator Hugo Black of Alabama standing on the steps. A light rain had begun to fall; the senator was looking for a taxi. She offered him a ride to Capitol Hill in her White House limousine.

Senator Black, though he was reputed once to have been a member of the Ku Klux Klan, had been a strong supporter of the New Deal in the Senate—which it was not politically easy for an Alabaman to do—and the President felt a warm friendship for him.

The senator was a tall man, his black hair rapidly retreating, with a long, thoughtful face.

"Well, Senator, have I been a bad girl?" asked Mrs. Roosevelt when they were seated in the back of the car.

She was referring to a visit she had paid to a reformatory for girls, where she had sat down with the girls at their lunch table. A photograph of the First Lady with the uniformed inmates of a girl's reformatory had appeared in many newspapers. Since most of the girls were Negroes, a few southern newspapers had thundered editorially.

"You know," said Senator Black, "Abraham Lincoln never really said, 'You can fool all of the people some of the time and some of the people all of the time, but you can't fool all of the people all of the time.' He never said it. Anyway, what he should have said was, 'You can please all of the people some of the time and some of the people all of the time, but you can't please all of the people all of the time.' It isn't even worth trying."

The First Lady nodded and smiled. She looked out the window and saw that the drizzle had turned to rain. Umbrellas were going up. People scurried for shelter.

"Let me change the subject, Senator Black," she said. "You know Mr. Paul Duroc was murdered in the Executive Wing last week. Poisoned. Miss Thérèse Rolland is accused. Did you know either of them? I mean, being a southern senator, you might—"

"Huey Long and I were not friends," said Senator Black firmly. "I'm a southern senator, but I didn't have to associate with that guttersnipe demagogue."

Mrs. Roosevelt grinned. "That's plain enough."

"The way he pawed that young woman in the presence of other men was alone enough to earn my contempt—for both of them. If you want to know something about Paul Duroc, I suggest you talk to Samuel Paxton."

"Who is Samuel Paxton?"

"He is a lobbyist for the Mississippi Riverboatmen's Association—MRA. He told me about a month ago that he gave Paul Duroc ten thousand dollars for the Huey Long presidential campaign fund. He gave that money only about a month before Huey died. He thinks his association is entitled to have it back. He demanded it of Duroc. Duroc just laughed at him."

"I've heard he was Senator Long's bag man."

The senator grinned, surprised perhaps at the First Lady's use of the slang term. "Samuel Paxton is an angry man. He is not accustomed to being laughed at. In past years, the Republican years, he was one of the most influential men in Washington."

"This is most helpful, Senator. We've been trying to get a lead ever since last week. It is altogether too simple, you see, just to assume Miss Rolland poisoned Paul Duroc. The case against her is so simple, in fact, that I find its very simplicity suspicious. Miss Rolland may have had ample motive to kill Mr. Duroc—though I can't imagine what that motive might be—but she would hardly have been so stupid as to shut herself up in an office with him and administer the poison when no one else could have done it."

Senator Black shook his head. "I like your logic," he said, "but you have just mentioned the hole in it."

"When I said—?"

" 'No one else could have done it.' "

"Hello, Uncle," said Kennelly. Speaking to Alfred Schmidt, he used the word *uncle* because it was the term commonly applied to pawnbrokers. It was not flippant; it was just what pawnbrokers were called. "Kennelly. D.C. police."

Schmidt was the very caricature of a pawnbroker: old, small, wizened, hunched, staring up over the frames of his round, gold-rimmed glasses. His shop on Fifteenth Street was everybody's image of a pawnshop: cluttered with every imaginable kind of wares, from firearms to musical instruments to dishes to tools.

"Kennelly . . ." he mused. "Kennelly. Yes. We have met before." He looked at the gold badge. "A lieutenant already! You don't remember me, do you, Kennelly?"

Kennelly frowned. Then he nodded. "Was it 1928?"

"No, it was 1927," said Schmidt. "You were in uniform then, Kennelly. Patrolman Kennelly. Corporal Kennelly . . . You thought I was an evil man. But—" He shrugged dramatically. "I took a Colt automatic in pawn. I reported the serial number to the police department. Also the name of the man who pawned it. It wasn't redeemed, I sold it. I reported again. Can I help it the man who bought it shot his father-in-law with it? Is it the fault of an automobile salesman that the man he sells a car uses it to rob a bank?"

"We were younger then, Uncle."

"You were. I've always been an old man. Maybe sometime I wasn't. I don't remember. What can I do for you, Kennelly?"

"You clean gold jewelry. Also silver. A radical cleaning process, no?"

"A *dangerous* cleaning process. But a ring that's worth ten dollars, so badly scratched, I make worth fifty dollars. Someday it'll kill me."

"What do you use?"

"Cyanide of potassium. You want to die? Put a little on your finger and stick it in your mouth."

"I'm investigating a murder where somebody died of cyanide poisoning."

"I don't sell the stuff."

"Did anybody ever steal any from you?"

"Why do you ask? You wouldn't be here if you didn't know."

Kennelly grinned. "Okay, Uncle. You reported somebody stole a can of potassium cyanide. Ten days ago. Right?"

"Right, exactly. It is dangerous, that. As soon as I discovered it missing, I called the police. Your investigating patrolmen thought I was a madman. Somebody stole a quarter of a cup of poison, they said. Somebody wants to kill rats."

"How much did they get, really?"

"Fifty milliliters. About two ounces. Enough to kill a company of soldiers."

"The report says it was stolen overnight."

Schmidt shrugged. "I told the officers I discovered it missing in the morning. It could have been stolen overnight, the day before, the night before that."

"Where was it?"

"In the back room. On a shelf. I had two cans, one open, one full. They took the full one."

"This place is carefully locked at night, isn't it?"

Schmidt nodded. "Unless you are a skilled burglar. My locks were not broken. Your men were not enough interested to look for scratches on the locks, or any of that. I looked. I could see no sign of force being used on my locks. I would say a set of skeleton keys was used. Or a good pick in the hands of a talented picker."

"Doesn't sound like you have very good locks," said Kennelly.

The hunched old pawnbroker shrugged. "To protect a stock of used guitars? I keep jewelry in the safe. Also firearms—that is, the pistols. I run chain through the trigger guards of shotguns and rifles and chain them to the pipes. Since last week I keep the cyanide in the safe."

"To steal your cyanide," said Kennelly, "someone had to know you had cyanide and where you kept it, open your locks, and come in and get it."

"Which is a lot of trouble," said Schmidt, "to get what you can buy cheap."

"Where do you buy it?"

"I buy it from McAllister Supplies on D Street. I have to call them first, because they don't stock it. I buy fifty milliliters about twice a year."

"How much fuss to get them to sell it to you?"

Schmidt shook his head. "It's like the way I report firearms. They keep a ledger book. You buy cyanide, you sign for it. I don't know what'd prevent you signing fake."

"Do they ask what business you're in, what you want with potassium cyanide?"

"No more. They asked the first time I bought it, ten or twelve years ago. They gave me a big lecture about how dangerous the stuff was. I told them, 'Hey, I know what's poison. The stuff scares me.' "

"It is scary stuff, isn't it?"

"You bet. So you have to sign," said Schmidt. "You could sign fake. So maybe my cyanide has been used to commit murder, or maybe to poison rats."

"Or maybe to polish silver," said Kennelly.

The old pawnbroker used both hands to adjust his spectacles. "Look at that ring you're wearing, Kennelly. That's real gold, and it's a disgrace, the way you've let it get scratched. You trust me not to dissolve it?"

Schmidt led Kennelly into the back room of the pawnshop. He took a small can from the safe and carried it to a little sink. There he ran some water into a glass bowl and used a tiny spatula to pick up a minuscule quantity of white powder from the can. He used a spoon to stir.

"You know that's where it gets dangerous," said Kennelly. "The hydrogen cyanide—"

"I told you, I know about poisons, Kennelly," said Alfred Schmidt. "Give me the ring."

Kennelly handed over his heavy gold ring, token of his having served through all the offices and presided over a chapter of Knights of Columbus, years ago. Schmidt was right that the ring was drab now, dulled by years of scratchings and scourings.

The pawnbroker dropped the ring in the water. "Tea?" he asked. "It will take a minute."

"Thanks I— Well, actually . . . Sure."

"I never poisoned anyone accidentally," said the little old man with an elfin smile.

A copper kettle was already steaming over a low gas flame. Schmidt poured tea leaves into a china pot. He let it steep for a minute or two, while Kennelly glanced uneasily from time to time at his ring. Schmidt poured the tea through a strainer, into two cups.

"Want to choose your cup?"

Now Kennelly could chuckle. "I trust you," he said.

The pawnbroker did not offer sugar, milk, or lemon but the tea was good, strong and good. Kennelly had never drunk it that way, but resolved he would again.

After a few more minutes, Schmidt put the bowl in the sink and ran water into it. He ran water for a full minute, until the bowl and ring were thoroughly rinsed and all the deadly poison had gone down the drain.

He handed Kennelly the ring. "See?"

The ring gleamed as it had on the day when the members of the lodge presented it. Like new.

Schmidt shrugged. "I wanted you to see I had a legitimate purpose in having the deadly poison in my shop."

"I believed you," Kennelly said.

"No other pawnshop does this," said Schmidt. "In fact, there are only two more pawnshops in Washington, as you probably know. Small-time, not like me. I'm the only real pawnbroker in town. Two jewelers clean with cyanide, I think. It's not a good idea if you're the careless type—" He shrugged. "You can kill yourself."

It was the kind of question she would have directed to Louis Howe. He would have known who Samuel Paxton was, and all about him. But Louis was beyond being troubled with that kind of question now. Even if she were going to see him today, Mrs. Roosevelt would not have asked him the question.

Jim Farley. Jim had been the campaign chairman in 1932 and was again this year. It was his business to know who everyone was. She placed a call to him. He was Postmaster General.

"Hello, Eleanor. What can I do for you?"

"Tell me what you know about a man named Samuel Paxton."

"Sam? Old-line lobbyist. He's represented several industrial groups over the years. Right now his chief client is the Mississippi Riverboatmen's Association."

"Is that an important lobbying client?"

"You bet it is. The government spends many millions of dollars every year keeping the channels open on the Mississippi, maintaining the navigation lights and markers, and so on. Sam works hard to see the appropriation is big enough to do the job."

"I understand he is—or was—a leading Republican."

"A successful lobbyist has to be to some degree nonpolitical."

"I suppose he puts money around."

"He'll put some our way this year."

"I've heard that he gave some money to Paul Duroc, for Senator Long's presidential campaign fund. I've heard that when Senator Long was assassinated, Mr. Paxton asked that the money be returned. I've heard it was not returned."

"If you're looking into the Duroc murder, you should have asked me about this sooner, Eleanor. I'm coming over to have cocktails with Frank this evening. Could we meet first?"

"Would you mind if a Secret Service agent were present? Would you mind if a D.C. police detective were present? I should like for them to hear what you have to say."

"Why not? I'll tell you something, Eleanor. Terry Rolland didn't kill Duroc. It's a setup. There are plenty of men with motives to kill Paul Duroc. We'll talk about it."

James A. Farley, Chairman of the Democratic National Committee and Postmaster General of the United States, was an acknowledged political genius. He had made an immense contribution to the successful campaign of 1932.

Crossing and recrossing the country, he promoted the Roosevelt candidacy with all his energy. Possessed of a phenomenal memory, he had stood at the side of Governor Roosevelt at a hundred train stops and had quietly advised the candidate of the names and affiliations of every politico approaching with outstretched hand—making it possible for the Governor to smile warmly and say things like, "Well, hello there, George! How are things at the Chamber?" and "Les, I've been thinking about what you said to Jim about the aluminum problem."

Farley knew not just who was who, but whose hand was in whose pocket.

A bald, bulky New York Irishman, he had endeared himself to the nation's stamp collectors by issuing kinds of stamps Americans had never seen before, not just repeated portraits of presidents, but beautiful stamps, many printed on collectors' sheets and not meant to be used as postage. Some commemorated events in American history. A particularly beautiful set featured exquisite engravings of scenes from the national parks. When congressmen complained to Farley that the "artistic" stamps were expensive to print, he laughed at them and pointed out that millions of postage stamps were bought and put in collectors' books—meaning that the Post Office Department did not have to deliver mail for that postage.

He needed no introduction to Stan Szczygiel; he remembered him. He shook Ed Kennelly's hand and said he was happy to meet him.

Mrs. Roosevelt went directly to the point. "Mr. Paul Duroc was—?"

Farley shook his head. "If Huey Long had not been assassinated, he would have mounted a major campaign against

Frank in the Democratic primaries, or would have formed a third party, or both, and would have drained off millions of votes that Frank should have this November. Huey was a megalomaniac. His ambition knew no limit. He was collecting a war chest. Only his way of collecting a war chest was different from anything *we* ever did."

"In what way, specifically?" asked Mrs. Roosevelt.

"His collectors were entitled to a commission," said Farley. "Ten percent, ordinarily. That's how he motivated them."

"All right. But Paul Duroc—"

"Took more than ten percent. And had his own special methods of collection."

"Like . . . ?"

"Let's talk about boats on the Mississippi, since that was the starting point for this conversation. What do you suppose might happen to a towboat shoving twenty barges down the river in a fast current on a rainy night if . . . If not only did a navigation light go out but a different one showed up along the Louisiana shore, a hundred yards, two hundred yards from where that light was supposed to be?"

"Extortion," said Szczygiel.

Farley nodded. "Huey could kill a bill. Most of the senators hated him, but under the rules of the Senate he could kill a bill. He'd talk it to death. If it was a minor bill, not a part of the administration's program, the Senate would just give up. But that minor bill might mean a hell of a lot to somebody."

"And Duroc was his bag man for that kind of thing?" asked Kennelly.

"Duroc was *one* of his bag men. A lobbyist who wanted

Huey to sit down and shut up would go see Duroc. *Come* to
see him, here at the White House."

"He was running this kind of operation *out of the White
House*?"

"Where better?"

Kennelly blew a loud sigh. "A woman was living in
Duroc's house. Since his death, she's disappeared. Do you
have any idea who she might be?"

"Check the whorehouses," said Farley. "His taste in
women was . . . catholic—with a small 'c.' "

"Terry Rolland?" asked Kennelly

"A small-timer," said Farley. "Huey used her. I don't
know what the attraction was, but I can imagine, and I
don't want to talk about it. I don't think she killed him,
Eleanor. Terry may be small-time, but she's not naive. She's
been around. She's not a woman who'd kill a man from
outraged sensibilities."

"Suppose he had found irregularities in her accounts?"
asked Mrs. Roosevelt.

Farley turned down the corners of his mouth and shook
his head. "Suppose he had. For irregularities that might
have cost her a year in the pokey—and you know she's had
a little experience being in the pokey, so it couldn't exactly
terrify her—she would go into a man's office alone with
him, close the door, and kill him? Huh-uh. I don't think so."
He turned toward Kennelly. "It's too pat, too easy. Put it
another way. It's too stupid. Terry Rolland is not that stupid."

Kennelly frowned deeply. "Y've got a point there, Mr.
Farley. Y've got a point."

VII

"I am not surprised to see you, Lieutenant Kennelly. Indeed, I had rather supposed I would see you before now."

It had been agreed that Mrs. Roosevelt should make no contact—at least not the initial contact—with the lobbyist Samuel Paxton. It was better, James Farley had also agreed, if Paxton first had a visit from a police officer. Kennelly had made no appointment. He had considered it better just to appear at Paxton's office.

Samuel Paxton was a formidable man. Like J. P. Morgan, he must have meant to be intimidating, must have practiced glowering. His head was big and solid, with thick white hair along the sides and in back, a gleaming dome in front and on top. He wore a great white mustache with points turning up. A gold-framed pince-nez rode the bridge of his nose, attached to the buttonhole in his lapel by a thin black silk ribbon. When he scowled, deep wrinkles appeared in his chin.

"Why did you expect to see me, Mr. Paxton?"

"Come now, Lieutenant. Let's not play games," Paxton said in a voice that was low and rough, yet resonant. "I expressed myself publicly to the effect that I detested Paul Duroc. When I heard he was dead, I said, 'Good! I'm glad to hear it.' Talk like that had to come to the attention of detectives investigating his murder. That makes me a suspect, does it not?"

"Actually no, Mr. Paxton. Actually I hadn't thought of you as a suspect. I thought of you more as a source of information."

Paxton lifted his big white eyebrows and let his pince-nez fall to the end of its ribbon. "Think of me as a suspect, Lieutenant Kennelly," he said. "Of course, I wasn't in the White House or anywhere near it on the day when Duroc died. But think. If I wanted to kill him, I would not have done it myself; I would have hired someone."

"Who would you have hired, Mr. Paxton? Do you know someone who'll kill for money?"

Paxton smiled for the first time. "I think if I offered you enough money, *you* would have done it for me, Lieutenant. That's not a comment on you personally, just a statement of my cynical view of mankind. I happen to believe people can be bought. I can't think of half a dozen people who can't be."

Kennelly did not care to debate the lobbyist on his cynical philosophy. He shrugged and shook his head.

Paxton offered a cigar from an ebony box. Kennelly accepted. While both of them were absorbed in lighting their cigars, Kennelly glanced around the office. Paxton sat behind his mahogany, leather-topped desk in a tall leather chair: a straight chair, not a reclining or swivel chair. No papers showed on his desk. Kennelly guessed that whatever papers were there were contained in the leather-covered boxes that occupied the sides of the desktop. Oddly, Samuel Paxton had two telephones on his desk. Kennelly wondered why. He could only talk on one at a time.

"What can you tell me that might help me identify the murderer?" Kennelly asked when he had his cigar going. He grinned and added, "Of course, if I arrest and convict the killer, then you'll no longer be a suspect."

"Paul Duroc," said Samuel Paxton calmly, "was a liar, a swindler, a cheat, an extortionist, probably a blackmailer, certainly an embezzler and thief—the perfect man to work for Huey Long."

Kennelly was taken aback by how this man could speak so vehemently, such hard words, without raising his voice or in any way losing his composure. He stated his charges against Paul Duroc as if they were incontrovertible facts.

"How much did he steal from you, Mr. Paxton?"

"He stole ten thousand dollars from my clients," said Paxton.

"Actually, you gave it to him as a campaign contribution, then asked it be returned after Huey Long was killed."

Paxton nodded. "Which he refused to do. He kept the money. He didn't turn it over to the Long machine in Louisiana."

"How do you know that?"

"I talked to Emile Baker in Baton Rouge."

"Who is Emile Baker?"

"The treasurer. He told me Duroc had held back a lot more money than mine."

"Giving still more people motive to want him dead," said Kennelly.

Paxton puffed on his cigar and nodded.

"What about Thérèse Rolland?" Kennelly asked.

"She didn't kill Paul Duroc," said Paxton bluntly.

"What makes you so sure?"

"She is a bit of fluff."

"She is a university graduate," said Kennelly. "She had a responsible job in the White House."

Paxton shrugged contemptuously. "I have seen her dance in her underwear, Lieutenant Kennelly."

For a moment Kennelly stared at his cigar. It was a good cigar, expensive—too expensive a habit to be acquired by a lieutenant of the District police. "A woman lived with Duroc," he said. "Would you have any idea who?"

"Thérèse Rolland, I should think—after Huey Long died."

"But it wasn't Terry Rolland."

"It could have been a lot of women. Duroc was fond of women."

"We found the key to a safe-deposit box. Would you have any idea where he did his banking?"

"No."

Having not been to the jail to visit Terry since Saturday, Mrs. Roosevelt felt an obligation to go there. Stan Szczygiel drove her to police headquarters, and a sergeant led her back to the cell range.

Terry stood and leaned against the bars.

"I didn't come here to interrogate you," said the First Lady. "I came to tell you I am still not convinced you are guilty. Indeed, I am all but totally convinced you did not kill Paul Duroc. The best news for you right now, Terry, is that some others are coming to the same conclusion."

"Is there any chance I can get out of here?"

"Not for the moment. I brought fruit and candy, also some books and more crossword puzzles."

Terry sat down on her cot. "Thank you, Ma'am. Thank you for makin' it possible for me to see my daddy outside." She sighed. "I'm grateful, but . . . y' know, he's been in jail himself. He called me a whoah."

"You're not," said Mrs. Roosevelt.

Terry shrugged. "Whut difference?" She sighed. "In these cells up and down the line here, we got whoahs, drunks, a shoplifter, a woman who beat her kids. I'm one of 'em."

"You don't belong here, Terry."

"I *am* here."

Mrs. Roosevelt wiped her forehead with a white-gloved hand. "We don't have another suspect. That's the trouble. I was told yesterday that there could be scores of people who hated Paul Duroc enough to want him dead; but we don't have a suspect. A woman was living with him in his house. Do you know who?"

"Talk about a whoah. Probably that was what she was."

"Let's be more serious, Terry. If we could find that woman, we might get information that would help get you out of here."

"He came in the office sometimes smelling of a perfume called Cinq Fleurs. It's imported from France. I recognized the smell because a French Quarter friend of mine in N'Orleans favored it and wore it all the time."

" 'Five Flowers,' " said Mrs. Roosevelt. "Actually, you know, it's not French. It's from the House of Floris, in London. It's exquisite—and also expensive."

"Doesn't mean she's a lady," said Terry. "Maybe he gave it to her. Maybe it was to *his* taste, more than hers."

"A very great deal of money is missing," said Mrs. Roosevelt.

"Not necessarily," said Terry. "Huey's only been dead six months, don't forget."

"What do you mean by that?"

"It isn't necessarily true that Paul lifted money out of the campaign chest. Maybe there wasn't much in the fund. Maybe Huey had been withdrawing it himself."

"Stealing from his own campaign funds?"

"Did he really want to run for President?" Terry asked. "Knowin' he didn't have a chance? Or was he just pretendin' he was goin' to run, to see how much money he could pick up from contributors?"

The First Lady frowned and slowly nodded. "We are being told that Senator Long was very . . . How shall I say it? That he was most *intimate* with you."

Terry drew a deep breath. "Huey did anything he wanted to do with me," she said. "Is that plain enough? If I'd wanted to kill somebody, it would have been Huey Long."

"Do you bet on horses, Terry?"

"Yes."

"Are you in debt to a bookie?"

"No. Well . . . For fifty dollars, somethin' like that."

"Would you like to tell me the name of your bookie?"

Terry shook her head. "That could get me in more trouble: givin' the cops the name of my bookie. Those guys got a long reach! Anyway, the fact that I bet on horses hasn't got anything to do with why I'm in here."

"You don't make it any easier for yourself."

Terry returned to the cell bars and gripped them in both hands. "You said it's gettin' clearer I didn't do it."

"But one problem remains," said Mrs. Roosevelt.

"Which is?"

"No one has yet discovered any way that anyone but you *could* have done it."

When Mrs. Roosevelt left the jail, Ed Kennelly was waiting for her, as was Stan Szczygiel.

"Odd thing's happened," Kennelly said. "Two guys broke into the boardinghouse where Terry has a room. They ransacked that room. They tore everything apart. The landlady, Mrs. Dugan, heard them and went in to see what was going on. They grabbed her, tied her up, gagged and blindfolded her, and left her on the floor while they went about their business."

Mrs. Roosevelt returned to the White House. She had appointments. Anyway, it would not have been wise for her to be seen at the boardinghouse. Kennelly and Szczygiel went to see the damage.

Mrs. Alice Dugan, who had been taciturn on Friday, was voluble now. "Who *is* that woman? What kind of trash does she associate with?"

"She doesn't associate with any kind of trash," said Kennelly. "The word that she's in jail was in the newspapers, so a couple of guys decided to see what they could loot from her room."

"She's in jail for *murder*!"

"Murderers are the very finest type of criminals," said Kennelly. "No riffraff, murderers."

"Anyway, she's only *accused* of murder," said Szczygiel. "She may be innocent."

Mrs. Dugan was a thin woman: thin face, thin body. She wore a black dress. "Who's gonna pay for this damage?" she asked, looking at the ruin of her room.

The room had been torn apart. The mattress had been slit with a knife, the pillows cut open and the feathers scattered. The upholstered chair had been gashed and ripped. Drawers and their contents were scattered on the floor. Clothes had been ripped.

Mrs. Dugan had been bound with strips of fabric torn from Terry's clothes. "Right there. On the floor. They said they'd knock me out if I tried to get loose. As soon as I knew they were gone, it only took me a minute to get loose."

"Did you get any idea what they were looking for?" Kennelly asked.

"No." The woman looked around the room and shook her head. "Whatever it was, it must have been important to them."

Mrs. Roosevelt left the White House at noon. She was driven to the Mayflower Hotel, where she was to attend a private showing of the new Charlie Chaplin film, *Modern Times*. A few prominent Washingtonians would see the picture besides the First Lady: Vice President John Nance Garner, Secretary of Labor Frances Perkins, Senators William Borah and Carter Glass, some local newspaper reporters, and— oddly and unhappily—Director of the FBI J. Edgar Hoover, who had asked to view the film because he had heard it was Communist propaganda and wanted to see for himself.

The first event of the showing was a reception, at which news cameramen were allowed to take their photographs of the celebrities. Chaplin himself was, of course, their favorite, followed by his wife, the actress Paulette Goddard. The best shot, the photographers all agreed, was a picture of the diminutive Chaplin with the tall First Lady.

Out of character, without his makeup and costume as the

Little Tramp, Chaplin was not immediately and easily recognizable. His face was almost bland, except for the keen, pensive eyes that no other actor could even imitate.

"I have enjoyed your work immensely, Mr. Chaplin," Mrs. Roosevelt said to him when she finally had a chance to speak a quiet word with the actor and comic.

"Thank you," he said.

"I believe I have profited from your work," she said.

His brows rose. "I know I have from yours," he said.

Vice President John Nance Garner joined the conversation—he of the flushed face, the wildly bushy white eyebrows with shrewd narrow eyes peering out from below. The butt of a cigar smoldered in the right corner of his mouth. His breath carried a faint sweet suggestion of the bourbon he had undoubtedly drunk before he arrived.

"I do enjoy y' pictures, Charlie," he said.

"I enjoy yours, Mr. Vice President," said Chaplin.

The Vice President hesitated a moment, then realized that Chaplin referred to the newspaper pictures that often appeared, and laughed heartily. Many photojournalists found it slyly amusing to take pictures of the old Texan looking foolish—which often happened when the Vice President was in no sense *being* foolish; he was simply the opposite of photogenic.

Garner seized Chaplin's hand and shook it warmly. "And y' lady," he said. "Miss Goddard—Miz Chaplin—it's a pleasure to see you, too."

They nibbled some of the hors d'oeuvres spread out on plates on a flower-laden table and sipped champagne. After a few minutes someone announced they would now go into the screening room and view the picture. Chaplain said a few words and offered a toast to his guests. Mrs. Roosevelt returned a toast to him and his wife.

The film, *Modern Times*, featured the Little Tramp as an industrial worker caught up in the drudgery of the assembly line. In one scene he and another worker appeared to have been eaten by the immense gears of a huge machine. In earlier Chaplin films the theme had often been a little man's struggle against enormities visited on him by bigger men. In *Modern Times* the indignities inflicted on the Little Fellow were even worse, since they were imposed by the machines, by the system. In other films he had fought, outwitted, escaped the bully. He could not shrug off the machine with a flick of his cane, a tip of his hat, or even a kick in the pants. The machine was invulnerable to humanity.

The film was powerful, and Mrs. Roosevelt was touched.

After they left the screening room, Senators Borah and Glass took Chaplin aside to speak with him. Mrs. Roosevelt chatted with Vice President Garner while she waited for a moment to give a brief word of congratulation to Chaplin before she left.

J. Edgar Hoover joined them.

"Well, Director Hoover, did you enjoy the film?" the First Lady asked.

"I'm not sure it isn't a thinly veiled attack on some important American values."

The Vice President shook his head as he sucked fire into a fresh cigar. "Aw, grow up, Jack," he said to John Edgar Hoover.

Returning to the White House, Mrs. Roosevelt found a note asking her to telephone Allen Layman, the Treasury Department auditor who was reviewing Paul Duroc's files. An hour later, she had time for him, and Layman came to her office.

"I'm afraid I've found discrepancies in Miss Rolland's accounts," he said.

"I'm sorry to hear that," said Mrs. Roosevelt.

The white-haired, wrinkled auditor opened a file on his lap. "Yes," he said. "Discrepancies. For example . . . On various dates last year and early this year, she entered into purchasing contracts with a company called William P. Dutton and Company, suppliers of office furniture and equipment. Three of those contracts were for a sufficient amount of money that the applicable regulations required her to advertise for bids. She did not. She simply bought the furniture. When she put through the vouchers for payment of the accounts, she falsified the forms, indicating she had advertised for bids and that Dutton had bid low."

"Oh, dear."

"There are other discrepancies of the kind. Miss Rolland simply was not scrupulous in following government purchasing regulations."

"Is this terribly unusual, Mr. Layman?"

Allen Layman raised his eyebrows and sighed. "I'm afraid not. You will remember the old cliché to the effect that the king cannot do his business as cheaply as other men. The regulations are designed to enable the government to do its business as cheaply as private organizations. But— Well, in fact, bid-rigging is not at all unusual in private organizations. Many a company purchasing agent becomes a wealthy man."

"Have you any evidence that Miss Rolland was taking— What is the term?"

"Payoffs," said Layman. "Kickbacks is a new term. Bribes. No, I have seen no evidence of that. On the other hand, I am auditing Miss Rolland's government business, not her personal accounts."

Mrs. Roosevelt frowned and shook her head. "I must confess to you, Mr. Layman, that I was hoping you would find nothing of this sort. I am grateful to you for being so thorough, but I regret it that your conscientious work has discovered this distressing information."

"I've found more," said Layman, closing one file folder and opening another. "Paul Duroc was conducting his audits in a rather idiosyncratic way."

"Indeed?"

"Yes. In his filing cabinets I found a very thick file— hundreds of pages of documents and notes—having to do with an audit of the Bureau of Yards and Docks, Department of the Navy. As you may know, Mr. Duroc never made public a finding of any discrepancies in the accounts of the Bureau of Yards and Docks. Which is not to say he didn't find any."

"What sort of discrepancies?"

Allen Layman could not suppress a little smile that Mrs. Roosevelt could not but take as self-congratulatory. "In the Bureau of Yards and Docks they treat contract bids in the same cavalier way that Miss Rolland has treated them. The difference is that Miss Rolland's misconduct involved contracts for amounts no greater, in total, than five thousand dollars. The loss to the government, if her bids were rigged, could not be greater than, say, one thousand dollars. I mean, on the Dutton purchases. If someone else might have bid four thousand and Miss Rolland bought the furniture and equipment for five thousand—"

"Yes, I see your point," said Mrs. Roosevelt. "It could not have cost the government more than one thousand dollars."

"Last year, Ma'am, the Bureau of Yards and Docks contracted for the construction of a seaplane dock and ramp at Pensacola Naval Air Station. That construction cost the government four hundred and fifty-five thousand dollars. It was handled the same way Miss Rolland handled the Dutton account. No bids were taken, but the Bureau vouchers say they were taken. The construction work was done by a company called Summerfield Construction, Incorporated. We have to wonder how much that cost the government."

"What we have to wonder," said Mrs. Roosevelt caustically, "is what it cost Summerfield to silence the navy comptrollers and Mr. Duroc."

"What I wonder," said Layman, "is how many incidents of the kind there were during Duroc's tenure. David Elliott at REA refused to pay off, I would guess—so Duroc nailed him. Summerfield Construction paid, and Duroc closed the file."

"A lucrative way of extortion," said Mrs. Roosevelt thoughtfully. "I wonder if he did it for Senator Long or for himself."

"I'll make a guess," said Layman as he closed his second file. "While the senator lived, Duroc lived under his protection and turned over most of the money to him. When the senator died, Duroc tried to keep it up, but without the senator's protection it was only a matter of time until someone killed him."

"Do the files you're working on suggest who it might have been?"

"No. Not yet, anyway. I went through the most active files and found nothing that might tell us."

Mrs. Roosevelt pondered for a moment. "The solution has

to be in an active file, don't you think? In Miss Rolland's, or—"

"No," said Layman. "The solution may be in an old file, and the motive may be someone seeking revenge against an insolent extortionist. Or . . ." He shrugged. "He may have been killed by someone meaning to get hands on the money he must have accumulated."

"This one may be worth somethin', Lieutenant."

A detective named Lee Slusser sat facing Ed Kennelly in the lieutenant's office. He had spent part of two days checking out the subscribers to the telephone numbers they had found written on Terry Rolland's telephone book.

"I mean," Slusser continued, "you don't hardly figure the lady visited a barbershop. I went back and took a look at her in her cell. That hair wasn't cut by any men's barber."

"So?" asked Kennelly impatiently.

"So I went to McIntyre's barbershop and had my hair cut. Cost me fifty cents."

"Put in for the fifty cents," said Kennelly.

"Okay. Anyway, it's a one-man shop. While I was waiting and while he was cutting my hair, the phone kept ringing. The guy was booking horses. No question. He was booking horses. So, if you're looking for the lady's bookie, that's him. Stan McIntyre."

"I guess I'll have to go see him," said Kennelly.

"Yeah. Well . . . Let me give you something else. The guy sells numbers, too."

Kennelly guessed that McIntyre's barbershop would close at six. He was right.

"Sorry, fella," said the barber. "When I finish this customer here, I'm closin' for the day."

"It's all right," said Kennelly. "I just want to talk to you for a minute."

"So talk."

"I'll wait till your customer's gone," said Kennelly. He pulled down the blind on the glass door, showing the CLOSED sign printed on it, and he latched the door. He sat down and picked up a copy of *Police Gazette*.

The barber stiffened. For a moment he stared at Kennelly with an apprehensive frown. Then he went on cutting hair.

Stan McIntyre, barber, was a man in his fifties: small, thin, nervous-quick in his movements. His yellowish gray hair would have required little cutting; there was not much left of it. He wore round steel-rimmed spectacles, a white shirt with a tiny black leather bow tie, and white pants.

The barbershop was like every other. The wood floor was littered with hair. Scissors and razors stood in jars of pink antiseptic. The air was heavy with the smells of hair tonics that stood in a rank of bottles in front of the big mirror. A mirrored plaque on one wall proclaimed IT PAYS TO LOOK WELL. A gas space heater kept the little room warm.

The barber finished his customer, took his money, and let him out of the shop.

"No action this time of day," said Kennelly.

"Whatta ya talkin' about?"

Kennelly showed his badge. "Let's don't play games, Stan. One of my boys was in and had a haircut, saw and heard you booking horses. Plus numbers."

The barber lifted his chin and looked down at Kennelly with an expression of skepticism and defiance. "It's no secret," he said.

"In other words, you're payin' off," said Kennelly. "You're payin' somebody to turn a blind eye and let you run a book in the precinct." He smiled and shook his head. "Doesn't cut any ice downtown. I can rack your ass into a cell any time I want to, and the precinct will deny it ever heard of you. And by the time you get out, nobody *will* have ever heard of you. You wanta stay in business, you're gonna have to pay Kennelly. *Kennelly*, you understand?"

"Figures," mumbled the barber.

"Yeah, figures. Only you're not figurin' it right. I don't want a nickel out of you, Stan. I want information. I'm workin' on a homicide, and I want information. That's the price for running a book in this town: a cut to the precinct, information to headquarters. So— I have some questions. I could use a haircut."

Kennelly shrugged out of his topcoat and hung it on the rack, together with his hat. He climbed into the barber chair, and Stan McIntyre pinned the paper collar around his neck and spread the cloth over him.

"Read the papers, Stan?"

The barber nodded as he lifted his clippers from their sterilizing bath and wiped them dry with a towel.

"Notice that one of your bettors is in jail and charged with murder?"

Stan McIntyre sighed. "Terry Rolland," he said.

"Right."

"She didn't do much business. Only now and then. What's the word? Sporadic."

"How much is she into you for, Stan?"

The barber shook his head. "Say, fifty bucks. Somethin' like that."

"She used the phone, huh?"

"Yeah. When she won, I mailed her dough. When she lost, she mailed it to me."

"What's the most she was ever into you, Stan?"

"Coupla bills. And I can't carry that much. I called her and told her she had to pay up. She did, in less than a week."

"Where'd you call her?"

"At her office. She worked at the White House. She gave me a code name. I had to tell the White House operator that Mr. Brady was calling. She'd left instructions with the operator always to put Mr. Brady through."

"How good was she?" Kennelly asked.

The barber, who was now working his clippers along the side of Kennelly's head, grinned and asked, "How good are any of them? Nobody wins, in the long run."

"How much was she losing, on average?"

"Well . . . Say twenty dollars a week. Seventy-five or eighty a month."

"Her job at the White House paid her a hundred and eighty dollars a month," said Kennelly.

The barber shook his head. "I don't go out and recruit bettors, Lieutenant. I just book their bets."

"You say she's into you for half a C-note?"

"Right. About that."

"Well, don't figure on collecting very soon, Stan," said Kennelly. "My guess is, she won't be on the street for some time."

As Kennelly left the barbershop, he was confronted on the sidewalk by a uniformed police captain: the precinct captain.

"What's the problem, Kennelly?" the captain asked. "You

hasslin' McIntyre? You ought to know better. You want to hassle somebody in my territory, you check with me first."

"Back off, O'Neill," Kennelly grunted. "Protection you sell out here doesn't count downtown."

"I'm your superior officer, Lieutenant," said the captain. "You call me sir."

Kennelly grabbed the captain's silver badge, ripped it off his coat, and threw it as far as he could, across the street, into the gutter opposite. He snatched off the captain's hat, threw it on the sidewalk, and ground it under his shoe. Then he drove a fist into the captain's swollen gut. The captain grunted and bent over, clutching his stomach and trying to hold down vomit.

"Understood, *Sir*?" Kennelly asked.

VIII

Wednesday morning began on a grim and melancholy note for Lieutenant Ed Kennelly. He was reminded that the murder of Paul Duroc was not the only homicide case that had claim to his attention. He was called to the morgue at nine to view a body that had been found on the street shortly before dawn.

The body lying naked on the stainless-steel table was that of a young woman: exceptionally beautiful, with black hair, brown eyes, a complexion oddly pallid, even for a body that had lost a lot of blood, a lovely body unscarred except for the entry wounds of three bullets that had penetrated her chest. The body had been found lying in the gutter on the south side of F Street, eleven blocks east of the White House and four blocks west of Union Station—ironically, just east of the court buildings on Judiciary Square.

Lee Slusser, the same detective who had checked the telephone numbers and found the barber, had done the preliminary work on this case.

"You're gonna love this one, Lieutenant," he said. "No ID. Nothing on her to suggest who she might be. Some little puncture holes in her arms, the kind you find on people who use dope. Fingerprints— Not on record. She was not sexually abused. And—get this—whoever killed her didn't lift the two hundred eighty-one bucks and sixteen cents she was carrying in her purse."

"When did she die?" asked Kennelly.

"The doc says about four this morning. A milkman driving by saw the body, got out to look, and called. The neighbors don't seem to have heard the shots. At least we haven't found anybody who admits to having heard them."

Kennelly took one last look at the body, then nodded to the morgue attendant to pull the sheet back over it.

"What a goddamn waste," he said.

Back at headquarters, Slusser spread out on a table the contents of the young woman's purse:

- The cash he had mentioned, which he said had not been in a billfold or any other kind of container but had been in the bottom of the purse.
- A handkerchief saturated with perfume.
- A compact with mirror, powder puff, and powder; a lipstick, rouge, and mascara.
- A small vial of a perfume labeled "Clinq Fleurs."
- A door key, with nothing to suggest what door it opened.

"Where's her clothes?" Kennelly asked.

The clothes were more difficult to look at. They were soaked with blood. The young woman had died wearing a silk-lined muskrat fur coat with a thick fox fur collar. Her dress was navy blue silk. Under the dress she had been wearing a peach-colored silk teddy, nothing more. Strangely, she'd been wearing no stockings; her legs had been bare on this wintry night. Oddly, too, she had worn no hat. Her long black hair must have mingled with the fur of her coat collar.

Slusser shook his head. "Doesn't figure," he said. "No sex. No robbery. Why'd somebody kill her?"

"For what you didn't find," said Kennelly. "Two hundred and whatever-you-said dollars. I bet she was carrying more. And identification. And maybe something else somebody wanted. Or maybe— Or maybe she knew too much about somebody or something. Or— What kind of gun?"

"Ballistics says the marks on the slugs say it was a Baby Browning, twenty-five caliber," said Slusser. "That's why it took three shots, also why nobody heard it."

"Jesus . . ." Kennelly winced. "What a way to die! Those little slugs drill in tearing and burning, rupturing veins and arteries. But they don't hit with enough shock to knock a person out."

"Well . . . Dead center," said Slusser. "We don't know who she is. We've got no idea who killed her. Or why."

Kennelly turned down the corners of his mouth as he surveyed the dead woman's bloody clothes. "I've got a pretty good idea who she is," he said. "I don't know her name, but— I've got an idea or two about why she was killed. Who did it—" He shrugged unhappily. "I don't know."

Fingerprint comparison proved what Ed Kennelly had expected. The dead woman's prints were not in the files, but they matched the fingerprints found all over Paul Duroc's house. She was the woman who had been living with him. He took a photograph of her face to Terry Rolland's cell. Terry shook her head. "I've never seen her. I have no idea who she is. Are you going to tell me?"

"I can't tell you what I don't know," said Kennelly.

Terry shuddered. The picture did not show the woman's wounds, but it was obvious that the face was the face of a corpse. "When did she die? Was she murdered?"

"Yes. Last night."

"Well, you can't accuse me of that one."

Later in the morning, Mrs. Roosevelt, Stan Szczygiel, and Ed Kennelly sat in the First Lady's study, drinking coffee.

"I can show you the picture," said Kennelly, "but I see no reason why you have to look at it."

"I am not squeamish," said the First Lady. She sat at her desk, in a gray wool dress. She had been reading letters and dictating answers. "It is remotely possible I might know her."

Kennelly handed her the picture. She studied the face for a moment, and she shook her head.

"She is the woman who was living with Paul Duroc," he said. "But we don't know who she was."

Mrs. Roosevelt pressed her hands together before her chin. "You know . . ." she said, "this might justify your releasing Miss Rolland. Together, these two murders suggests a conspiracy."

"I thought of that. But we haven't found a way that anyone else got the poison to Duroc. It doesn't have to be someone else, you know. A conspiracy could involve Terry Rolland killing Duroc and someone else killing the woman."

"The case against Miss Rolland grows weaker," said Mrs. Roosevelt.

"I grant that," said Kennelly. "But if we turn her loose, she might run. Her family has criminal connections. They might—"

"The poor young woman is *in jail*," argued Mrs. Roosevelt.

"The way she has been handling government purchasing contracts may have earned her a little time in jail," said Szczygiel.

"It's not as if she was a jail virgin," said Kennelly. "She's been in before. She's doing all right. It won't hurt her."

Mrs. Roosevelt did not agree but dropped the subject.

"The most disappointing thing about Miss Rolland is that she has lied to us," she said. "Most simply, she said she never drank on the job but you found a bottle of bourbon in her desk. She withheld the information that she was imprisoned in Louisiana. She talked about what a fine, proud gentleman her father was, and we learn he has served two terms of imprisonment. Now we find that she has used improper bidding procedures for White House procurement contracts."

"We find out Duroc was a crook," said Kennelly. "We find out the town is full of people with motive to murder him."

"We find out that the amounts of money involved were enough to motivate a variety of people to commit murder," said Szczygiel.

"I think," said Mrs. Roosevelt, "it might be well if Mr. Szczygiel paid a visit to Dutton Office Supplies."

"From the moment I read she was in jail, I've been expecting somebody to show up," said William P. Dutton.

Stan Szczygiel looked around the big office-supply store. He had just heard an interesting statement. Why would Dutton have *expected* an investigator to show up? Some men unconsciously revealed far more than they wanted to reveal.

"I am not here because she is in jail," he said. "As you may understand, the Secret Service is an agency of the Treasury Department. I am inquiring into some apparent irregularities in the granting of purchasing contracts."

Dutton was not subtle about his relief. "Ah," he said. "I hope there has been nothing wrong with the contracts *I* have fulfilled."

"No one but you bid," said Szczygiel.

Dutton stiffened. "But I *did* submit bids," said Dutton. "I had no idea that no one else bid."

William Dutton bounced up and down on the balls of his feet, unconsciously, with the intensity that characterized salesmen. He was the owner and president of his company, as Szczygiel had confirmed before he came, and likely he had earned his success by being more earnest and driven than his competitors. He had started his business in 1927, Szczygiel knew, and to have survived through the Depression he had to be a shrewd and zealous entrepreneur. He was forty-five, Szczygiel guessed: bald, with the face of a Kewpie doll. His eyes ranged the floor of his store, as though he were looking for a customer likely to be more important than this one.

"Uhm-hmm," said Szczygiel. "You didn't know she didn't call for any other bids. Sure you didn't."

Dutton glanced at the card Szczygiel had given him, obviously to be reminded of his name. "Are you accusing me of bid-rigging, Mr. Szczygiel?" he asked.

"Mr. Dutton," said Szczygiel, "I couldn't make a case against you if my life depended on it. You, I imagine, submitted your bid in response to a mail invitation for bids. You submitted your bid, never guessing it would be the only bid submitted. Miss Rolland never told you there were no other bidders. Right?"

"Right," said Dutton eagerly.

Szczygiel nodded. "Yeah. On the other hand, I imagine you sold office furniture and equipment to other federal agencies. Not so? Now, if there were a pattern— You follow me? If you were the only bidder on other profitable contracts, then we'd have to wonder . . . The Treasury Department would wonder. And the Justice Department would wonder. A jury might think—"

"Mr. Szczygiel!"

"Might think . . . Hmmm?"

"Let's talk in my office. Can I offer coffee?"

"Uh . . . You have any gin handy?"

They sat down in Dutton's office, on the second floor, where a wide window overlooked the selling floor of the big store. Dutton did indeed have gin handy and poured some over ice for Szczygiel. He poured some for himself—more, Szczygiel guessed, to seem comradely than because he really wanted a drink.

"I lied to you, Mr. Dutton," Szczygiel said after he had put his hat on the corner of Dutton's desk and taken a sip of gin. "I am not really so much interested in the rigging of government purchase contracts—though I might feel obliged to report an exceptionally flagrant case to the Justice Department—as I am in the murder of Paul Duroc."

"I swear to you I know nothing about that."

"I suspect you don't. But there are some things you do

know. Thérèse Rolland was spending money she didn't earn as a contract administrator for the White House. Where was she getting it?"

"How would I know?"

Stan Szczygiel grinned at Dutton. "Did you know she spent time in prison in Louisiana for rigging purchase contracts for things like schoolbooks?"

"My God, no!"

"Oh, yes. And, of course, the crime is always committed the same way. The contract administrator awards the contract to a sole bidder, or a high bidder, in return for . . . a payoff."

Szczygiel was describing what he really only guessed about the way Terry Rolland had gotten herself sentenced to the Plaquemines Parish prison farm. It was good enough. As he said, the crime was always committed the same way.

"Mr. Szczygiel—"

"You didn't pay her much. The contracts weren't that big. But you—and I suppose some others—made it possible for her to lose seventy-five dollars a month betting on the horses."

"My God! She—"

"Not on her salary, Mr. Dutton," said Szczygiel. "She was supplementing her income. How much did you supplement it?"

Dutton closed his eyes for a moment. "I submitted honest bids, Mr. Szczygiel," he said quietly. "I don't think the government could have bought what I sold them any cheaper, for the quality. Of course . . . When you know you are the only bidder, you don't have to be aggressively competitive."

"How much, Mr. Dutton?" Szczygiel asked bluntly.

"How much . . . ?"

"Did you pay her?"

Dutton sighed. "Not much, really. Bijoux. Little gifts, given in a sort of playful spirit. A new twenty-dollar bill in our Christmas card. That sort of thing. No specific tit for tat. Well . . . Then something happened. She called and asked me for a loan. She used an odd expression. She said she needed two bills."

"So you paid her two hundred dollars," said Szczygiel. "That's not insignificant money."

"She called it a loan."

"Did you believe it was?"

Dutton shrugged.

The state of Ohio had failed to redistrict itself properly after the 1930 census and so elected a congressman-at-large: a representative who was elected on a statewide ballot, in addition to its twenty-odd district representatives.

The congressman-at-large from Ohio was Stephen M. Young, a peppery, exuberant Cleveland lawyer. This Wednesday morning, the President was awarding a presidential citation, and Congressman Young brought the honoree to the White House. The arrangement was that the citation would be personally awarded just before noon, after which the congressman and the honoree would join Mrs. Roosevelt and the Secretary of the Treasury for lunch.

Congressman Young fairly bounced into the Oval Office. "Mr. President!" he said. "Mrs. Roosevelt! Secretary Morgenthau! Let me introduce Eliot Ness!"

The famous treasury agent who had brought down Al Capone had recently been appointed safety director for the city of Cleveland. He was a nattily dressed man of medium build. His freckled face was memorable for his wide, toothy smile. He parted his abundant hair in the middle, and it swept over his forehead on both sides. He stepped forward and shook the President's hand, then extended his hand to the First Lady and to Henry Morgenthau.

"You and my wife should have a fine luncheon conversation, Mr. Ness," said the President. "She fancies herself something of a detective."

"I shall correct that misstatement over lunch," said Mrs. Roosevelt.

The President laughed. "I bet she asks you for some tips."

"Actually," said Henry Morgenthau, "a man was murdered here last week, right here in the Executive Wing, upstairs."

"In the White House?" asked Ness skeptically.

"In the White House, Mr. Ness," said Mrs. Roosevelt. "On the second floor, just above us."

"Not with a gun, I hope," said Ness.

"No. With poison. However, a man was shot right here in the Oval Office in 1934. The President was not in the Executive Wing at the time. It was at night."

"Well," said the President abruptly, "I wish I had time to join you for lunch. I expect your conversation will be more interesting than the one I'll have with the congressmen who are coming in to see me. But— Shall we let the newspaper boys in and award the citation?"

Mrs. Roosevelt was amused by the way Congressman Young managed to get himself into the photographs of the President handing the citation to Ness. She understood. It was politics. A congressman who could get into a picture with President Roosevelt and Eliot Ness could expect to see that picture in every newspaper in his district—which in this case was the entire state of Ohio.

Over lunch in the private dining room on the first floor of the White House, Eliot Ness asked about the murder. Mrs. Roosevelt explained the case.

"Tidy," said Ness. "But cyanide . . . I'd think that would be difficult to get."

"A District police detective has visited chemical supply houses," she told him. "He has shown them a photograph of Miss Rolland and also asked them for the names of any new purchasers—that is, people who never bought cyanide before. Also, a pawnshop where potassium cyanide is used to clean gold and silver reported a container of it stolen. So far, we have no clue as to who stole it, or why."

"Well, the President said I should give you a tip," said Ness, showing again his extraordinarily wide smile. "All I can tell you is, the secret is dogged police work."

"You're a legend, Mr. Ness. Is that how you became so?"

"That and a little luck. Also the good fortune to work under supportive Secretaries of the Treasury."

"Cleveland is fortunate to have you," said Mrs. Roosevelt.

"He's got one problem," said Congressman Young. "J. Edgar Hoover hates him."

"Why on earth would Mr. Hoover hate Mr. Ness?"

"Jealous of his reputation and of the publicity he gets," said the congressman. "John Edgar wants to be the nation's one and only top cop. He'll wait till Eliot gets Cleveland pretty well cleaned up, and then he'll move in with a team of FBI agents and try to claim credit. You just wait and see."

"He's got an ego as big as Capone's," said Ness dourly. "But he's not as smart."

* * *

Stan Szczygiel had given an assignment to a young Secret
Service agent, a newcomer to the White House named Dominic Deconcini. He'd had the young man check out the iden-
tities of every visitor to the West Wing on the afternoon of
Wednesday, March 4, the day when Paul Duroc was poisoned. Visitors signed a log in the lobby of the West Wing,
and some thirty-five people—other than staff—had come in
that afternoon. Since the task of checking thirty-five names
was time-consuming and the young man had other duties,
only a week later—*this* Wednesday—did he finish his report.

"Maybe I should have been more specific," said Szczygiel.
"Maybe I should have asked you to check only on people
who came in to visit Paul Duroc."

"Only two men signed in as visitors to Mr. Duroc that
afternoon," said Deconcini. "Congressman Stuart Devol
and Captain Richard Sykes."

"Who are they? Any information?"

"Yes, Sir. Congressman Devol represents the third congressional district of Florida, and Commander Sykes com-
mands the naval air station at Pensacola. Their names were
together in the log book, so I suppose they came in together."

"Is there anyone from Louisiana on the list?"

"Yes, Sir. Daniel Selmer. He was on Senator Long's staff.
He came in to see Mr. Oglesby. And Ernest McSweeney came
to see Vice President Garner. He's a lobbyist for the sugar
industry."

"Selmer stopped in to say good-bye," said Oglesby. "As if I
gave a damn. Said he's leaving Washington and was making
the rounds, saying his farewells. The only time he ever came

here when he didn't have some dishonest proposition to promote. A slimy man, Stan. The sooner the Long crowd is out of Washington, the sooner we can fumigate."

The Vice President's secretary said that McSweeney never did see Mr. Garner that afternoon. "The Vice President was supposed to be here by four-thirty, but he didn't show up until forty-five minutes later. Mr. McSweeney was nice about it. He said he'd see him later."

"Did he sit here waiting, all the time he was in the West Wing?"

"Oh, no. He wandered around. He knows everybody. He's been a lobbyist in Washington since 1912 or some such year."

Ed Kennelly stood in the morgue once more, gazing at the corpse of the woman who had now been tagged "Jane Doe."

"Honey, you were *somebody*," he said. He stared at her as if somehow the silent corpse could speak one more time, just a word. He stared as though he would see something he had overlooked when he saw her before. "Son of a *bitch*!"

"Lieutenant . . ."

"Slusser?"

"I went to the store where she bought the fur coat. The name was on the label, you know. Guess what. She bought the coat Monday. Got to wear it all of two days before she was shot in it."

Kennelly took Slusser by the arm, half to lead him out of the cold room of the morgue, half for support. "Now you're gonna tell me she paid cash, and you're gonna tell me they didn't get her name."

Slusser nodded. "Four hundred dollars. Cash. They asked

her name, and she said her name was Cash—meaning she did not choose to tell them."

"And of course she was a customer they'd never seen before."

Slusser chuckled. "She handed them eight fifty-dollar bills. They took the precaution of checking to see the serial numbers weren't the same."

"You took her photo to the precincts?"

"Right. Hey, what'd you do to O'Neill? The guy was mad as hell about something."

"I caught him lifting apples off a fruit stand," said Kennelly. "Handled it *my* way."

Slusser laughed. "You ruffled his feathers, Lieutenant."

"I don't give a damn. How are we going to identify Jane Doe?"

"We've done the usual. The morgue photo is on its way to Baltimore, Richmond, Philly, New York—"

"New Orleans," said Kennelly.

"Right, New Orleans."

"What about the labels in her other clothes?"

"No stores. But expensive names. I checked that. Jane Doe had money."

"Maybe only recently," said Kennelly.

"Okay," said Slusser. "Her compact—you know, the thing she kept her powder and powder puff in—was from Woolworth's."

"Four-hundred-dollar fur coat, silk dress, and a Woolworth compact. Got her money recently. Just hadn't got around to buying a more expensive compact. Where the hell you suppose she lived? Hotel?"

"Don't tell me I've gotta carry her picture around to hotels," said Slusser.

"Just the five or six most expensive ones. Try it. Just the five or six most expensive. She paid cash for her room, you can bet. In advance. Check with five or six hotels."

Stan Szczygiel faced Terry Rolland.

"Your friend Dutton has confessed," he said.

"Confessed to what?"

"To giving you two bills."

She swung away from the bars of her cell. "Shit! But . . . Hey, it doesn't prove anything about—"

"Duroc had a file on you," said Szczygiel. "That's where I got the name Dutton."

She took the three steps to the rear wall of her cell, then turned and came back to the bars. "It's got nothin' to do with anythin'," she protested.

"Sure it does," said Szczygiel. "He was blackmailing you."

"Fat chance! I didn't have any money."

"A woman can be blackmailed for other things besides money," said Szczygiel.

She gripped the bars and hung her head. "What you tryin' to do, Szczygiel? Hang me?"

"You're hanging yourself, Terry," he said, genuine sympathy—which she heard—in his voice. "You've lied." He shook his head. "Mrs. Roosevelt wants to think you're innocent. Y'know . . . Even Ed Kennelly wants to think you're innocent. So do I. Of murder. To cover your tracks as a petty thief, you're steering yourself into a murder conviction."

She drew a deep breath. "If he was blackmailin' me, there's your motive for murder."

Stan Szczygiel stood back from her and stared hard at the wretched young woman. "What you're guilty of, Terry, is utter, total, complete stupidity. If I were your lawyer, I'd argue that nobody could be so stupid as to lock herself in an office with a man, alone, and feed him the poison that killed him: circumstances that argue no one else could have done it. But you're just about that stupid, Terry. You're just about dumb enough to—"

"What do you want me to say?"

"All right. Was he blackmailing you?"

She nodded.

"For what?"

"Like you said. What a woman can pay. Huey's girl. It gave him a kick. Especially if he humiliated me. Huey humiliated him, and he was taking his revenge on Huey by—"

"I see the picture," Szczygiel interrupted.

"I didn't kill him!"

"Much as you might have liked to."

She closed her eyes and nodded. "Much as I might have liked to."

Szczygiel shook his head. "You won't make a very credible witness. A conviction for rigging bids in Louisiana. The same kind of thing here . . ."

"Hey . . . Dutton was the right company for the contract. I got good stuff at the right price, good service, quick replacement of anything that was bad . . . Hey! You have any idea what goes on in government purchasing contracts? Shoddy merchandise. Late deliveries. Stuff that doesn't meet the specifications. No replacement of defective merchandise. And for this . . . rigged bids, paybacks, inflated prices. I'm gonna be crucified for— *Paul* was gonna crucify me, or said he was, for— Szczygiel! Everybody does it!"

"I don't believe that's a defense at law," said Szczygiel dryly.

She closed her eyes and slumped against the bars of her cell. "What a damned mess . . ." she whispered.

Carrying the Jane Doe picture to hotels proved to be a less taxing job than Lee Slusser had supposed. She had been staying at the first hotel he checked: the Mayflower.

She had checked in on Thursday afternoon, March 5—one day after the death of Paul Duroc. She had brought only a small overnight case for luggage and had paid for her first night in advance, in cash. The next day, Friday, she came to the desk and said she would be staying a week. She paid for the week in advance, again in cash, two fifty-dollar bills.

The hotel had become a little concerned about having an attractive young woman staying alone and paying cash, and the house security man had watched her, to make sure she was not a prostitute, using her room to entertain her clientele. No one visited her, actually. She spent a good deal of time in her room. She ate most of her meals in the hotel.

Then, of course, the night before she had not returned.

Slusser looked at her signature on the register—"Elaine Curtis, 318 Broad Street, Columbus, Ohio."

"You want to see her room?" the house detective asked.

"I will," said Slusser. "But I don't want to go in until Lieutenant Kennelly arrives."

"Kennelly? Ed Kennelly? Homicide? You tellin' me the broad is *dead*?"

The President was pleased with his cocktail hour that evening. Besides Missy, who was always there, Pa Watson and Harry Hopkins sat and watched the President shake his pitcher of martinis.

"Does anyone have an opinion of the new Japanese cabinet?" the President asked.

It was unusual for him to inject such a question into cocktail-hour conversation. Obviously it was on his mind. The Japanese government had just been reorganized, with a new cabinet dominated by generals.

"They've announced a program for developing heavy industry," said Pa Watson. He was General Watson, the President's military aide—besides being a personal friend. "For 'heavy industry' read 'armaments industry.' They're going to accelerate the buildup of their army and navy."

The President nodded. "Now what in the world could Japan possibly want with a big army and navy?" he asked ironically.

"We don't have to speculate on that," said Pa Watson. "The only question is where? China, for sure. But maybe more. Maybe French Indochina."

"Well . . . Not much we can do about it," said the President, dismissing the subject.

Harry Hopkins grinned. "I've got a little funny to tell you," he said.

"I can always use a little funny," said the President.

"It's about your presidential citation this morning," said Hopkins. "About Eliot Ness. I had a call from Cleveland. You'd already announced the citation, so it was too late to do anything about it. Anyway, it's not so serious you'd have wanted to stop it, probably."

"This doesn't sound like the beginning of a funny," said Missy.

"Oh, it is, really," said Hopkins. "My friend in Cleveland thinks it's funny."

"Well, what is it?"

"It seems that the incorruptible Mr. Ness is not so incorruptible as to refuse small gifts," said Hopkins. "As Cleveland's top cop, he rides around town in a limo, eats in the best restaurants, drinks in the best bars . . . and never pays a check!"

The President laughed.

"No one suggests he takes bribes," Hopkins was quick to add. "He just seems to feel that free drinks and meals are a perquisite of his office."

"That *is* a funny," said the President. He laughed some more. "I wish I'd known this morning. I'd have given him the citation anyway, but it would have been a lot more fun if I'd known about this."

IX

Ed Kennelly arrived at the Mayflower Hotel within half an hour. Lee Slusser was waiting in the lobby, as was Gus Dorsey, the house detective.

"H'lo, Ed. Are we to understand our guest in 811 won't be coming back?"

"Hi, Gus. If the woman in 811 is the one whose picture Lee showed you, no, she won't be coming back."

Gus Dorsey was an overweight man in a tight black suit. His necktie was loose and tied wrong besides, so that the small end hung beneath the big end. "Keep it quiet?" he asked. "I mean, about her having a room here. Our guests don't need to know one of their fellow guests was murdered."

"Let's look at her room," said Kennelly.

There was not much to see. The hotel maids had followed their usual routine and had made the bed and replaced the towels. A small suitcase, empty, was in the closet. A red cloth coat hung in the closet, also two dresses and a sweater. A small supply of woman's underwear was in a bureau drawer—the same kind Kennelly had seen in Duroc's house near the zoo.

"Let me ask you a question, Gus," said Kennelly. "Do your guests carry their room keys, or do they drop them at the desk when they go out and pick them up when they return?"

"Most of them follow the American custom," said Dorsey. "Which is to carry their keys with them. The tags we put on keys aren't so big as to make them inconvenient to carry. I can tell you that Miss Curtis was carrying her key when she left here yesterday evening. I know because I checked to see how many keys to 811 we have behind the desk. Just one. That means she was carrying the other one."

"It wasn't found in her purse," said Kennelly.

"Dammit, we'll have to change the lock."

"From my point of view, I wish you had changed it already. Whoever killed her took the key from her purse, came here, entered this room, and took what I'd hoped to find."

"Which was?"

"Probably several thousand dollars in cash. Maybe the key to a deposit box. Also, everything that might have told us who she really was—'cause I don't believe for a minute she was Elaine Curtis from Columbus, Ohio. I'll check with Columbus PD, but I'm still calling her Jane Doe."

On her way out of the White House to a dinner engagement with a group of old friends from her days in Albany, Mrs. Roosevelt stopped by the Secret Service office at Stan Szczygiel's invitation. Ed Kennelly was there, too.

She was wearing her black coat and fox neckpiece. A

pheasant feather extended jauntily from her flat black hat.

The two men reported what they had learned since they met with her that morning.

"I'm sorry that I am in a hurry," she said. "Let me suggest there is a key to this mystery. If we are reluctant to believe Miss Rolland put the poison in Mr. Duroc's drink—and I believe that even you, Lieutenant Kennelly, have come to doubt she did—then we must find out how some other person did it. We know that Mr. Duroc had incurred animosities. What about the two Louisianans you mentioned, Mr. Szczygiel? Could they somehow have entered Mr. Duroc's office and—"

"We mean to talk to them, Ma'am," said Szczygiel.

"That's the key," said Mrs. Roosevelt emphatically. "We know Thérèse Rolland didn't kill Jane Doe. That suggests, though of course it doesn't prove, she didn't kill Mr. Duroc either. I suggest we focus on that. By what other means could the poison have been introduced into that bourbon and water? Something clever, I imagine. And I'm sure you know, gentlemen, the cleverest way of doing a thing is very often the simplest."

In the car on their way to dinner, Kennelly told Szczygiel he did not entirely agree with Mrs. Roosevelt. "Very often, the cleverest way to solve a problem is to come in through the back door. We might never find out who put the poison in Duroc's whiskey, by frontal attack. We may very well find out by chasing down the man who killed Jane Doe."

Over their dinner in an H Street restaurant where they ate Chinese food, Kennelly continued his argument.

"I've been mulling over an idea," he said. "We found a safe-deposit-box key taped to the bottom of a drawer of

Duroc's desk. We couldn't do a damn thing with it, because we didn't know what bank, what name. Okay. Suppose there was a second key. Not unusual. Holders of safe-deposit boxes often have two keys. If you were a guy who thought you might have to take it on the lam quick some-time, you might have two keys. So Duroc has the second key at home."

"I get you," said Szczygiel. "Jane Doe knows about the second key. When she hears Duroc is dead, she grabs that second key before she leaves the house."

Kennelly nodded. He glanced around the small, smoky Chinese restaurant, spotted their waiter, and summoned him. Chinese or no Chinese, he and Szczygiel were drinking American, and he ordered another round of drinks.

"Which," he said to Szczygiel, not missing a beat in the discussion, "could explain why a girl who has a Woolworth compact pays for an expensive fur coat with eight fifty-dollar bills and pays a week's room rent at the Mayflower in advance with fifty-dollar bills. Duroc's stash must be in a deposit box in her name."

"Which somebody figured, and they killed her to get the key," said Szczygiel.

Kennelly nodded.

"I can see why you didn't tell that to Mrs. Roosevelt," said Szczygiel. "She'd insist you release Thérèse Rolland."

"So far as I'm concerned, right now I'm holding her as a material witness," said Kennelly. "But she mustn't know that. She's got more to tell us. I don't think she killed Duroc. But she's crooked and smart. If we let her out, she'll blow. We'll never find her."

Szczygiel shrugged. "So what's next?"

"If you're game, I'm gonna take you a couple of places

where I want somebody to look at the pictures of Jane Doe."

Three-quarters of an hour later Kennelly parked his unmarked car on Sargent Road, in the northeast corner of the District of Columbia, not far from the Maryland line. He and Szczygiel walked half a block to a handsome Victorian home that sat on a little knoll above the road, half hidden from the street by tall old pine trees. They walked up weathered, flaking stone steps to the front porch and double doors.

"I think I know where I am," said Stan Szczygiel, a little apprehensive.

"It'll be on the house if we decide to buy . . . anything," said Kennelly.

The doorbell was rung with a key that spun clangers inside a big bell inside the door. The ring brought a Negro maid to the door.

"Please tell Blanche two gentlemen are here to see her."

The maid wore the blandest of all possible expressions as she nodded, then left them standing inside the door while she walked to the rear of the entrance hall and disappeared through a door.

They had only a minute to wait before Blanche appeared. She was taller than either of them and wore a floor-length skintight red silk dress over her spare figure. Her hair was unnaturally red: hennaed, the term was. A heavy smear of bright red lipstick seemed to thicken her lips. Her mascaraed lashes were like rows of little pins.

"Ed! *Nice* to see ya! Ya here on your business or mine?"

"Maybe both," said Kennelly. "Let me introduce my friend Stan Szczygiel. Stan's with the Secret Service."

"Do tell! Glad to meet ya, Stan."

"Got some good girls working tonight?" asked Kennelly.

"Let's see . . . You like Loretta, don't ya?"

"Sure do."

"Loretta's here. And I'm sure we can find somebody Stan'll like—unless he's got odd tastes."

Kennelly spoke to Szczygiel. "You game? We're in no big hurry."

Szczygiel shrugged, trying to look nonchalant. "Why not?" he said.

"Blanche . . . Before we go in, I'd appreciate it if you'd look at a picture."

"Uh-oh. Ya want me to finger somebody?"

Kennelly shook his head. "I want you to identify a stiff, if you can."

Blanche feigned a shudder. "A morgue photo? Well . . . Hope I don't whoop my cookies."

Just as Kennelly reached inside his overcoat to pull out the photograph, the double doors to the waiting room opened and two men came out.

The first interested Ed Kennelly. The fellow was middle-aged, with an undistinguished flat face, distorted into an expression of insolent brashness. His eyes met Kennelly's, then Szczygiel's. He seemed to want them to understand he had seen them, put them in his memory, and would remember them when he saw them again. What interested Kennelly was that when the fellow put his arms back to let the maid help him on with his overcoat, he showed the butt of a revolver hanging in a shoulder holster.

The second man was a paunchy boy, couldn't have been older than eighteen or nineteen.

Overcoats and hats on, the two men strode toward the door. The older one saluted Blanche but said nothing.

"Who the hell was that?" Kennelly asked Blanche.

"Ethics don't permit me to name my clients," she said. "Unless it's a police order."

"The guy's carrying a concealed weapon," said Kennelly.

"He's a bodyguard," said Blanche.

"For the young fellow?"

"Right. His name is Henry Ford. He's a grandson of *the* Henry Ford. The thug is Harry Bennett. The old man's in a hotel downtown and sent the boy out here for life lessons. It's the second time he's been here. The old man himself was a client, a few years ago. I've got a high-class clientele, ya know."

"You keep a high-class place, Blanche," said Kennelly. "Anyway, let me show you this picture."

Blanche stared at the photograph of Jane Doe's face, then shook her head. "Never worked for me," she said. "You think she was in this line of work?"

"No. Just a shot in the dark."

After they had stopped at two more houses, Szczygiel protested that this was interesting but getting them nowhere.

"Remember what Jim Farley said," Kennelly reminded Szczygiel. " 'Check the whorehouses.' Duroc's taste ran to hookers, he said."

"Invective," said Szczygiel.

"You have any better ideas? If we start checking bars, we could be at it a month."

Shortly before midnight they entered a house on N Street in Georgetown. The madam here was named Elizabeth and was usually called Bess. Her establishment was smaller than Blanche's, more modest, far less elegant. She invited Kennelly and Szczygiel into her candlelit sitting room.

Szczygiel wondered if the room was so dimly lighted to prevent clients from recognizing each other or to prevent their seeing the faults of the girls.

Bess pointed to the table where the candles burned. She herself sat down, and the two men sat at the table with her. She was a heavy woman who made no effort to hide her age, which was likely sixty. Her frizzled hair was dull black. Her plump cheeks were reddened with distinct spots of rouge.

Two of her girls sat on a couch on the opposite side of the small room. They wore crepe wrappers, which they allowed to lie partly open, as if carelessly. They had no idea who Kennelly and Szczygiel were, and when Szczygiel turned to look at them, they bared their breasts and grinned.

"What can I do for you, Lieutenant?" the madam asked.

"Official business, Bess," said Kennelly.

"Drink?" she asked, nodding toward the bottle of rye that sat on the table.

"Thanks, but we're trying to move fast tonight," said Kennelly. "I just want to ask if you know the girl in this picture."

As Bess looked at the morgue photo, she filled with breath and the corners of her mouth turned down. "She's dead. You're asking me to identify a corpse."

Kennelly nodded. "Murdered," he said.

The madam sighed. "Wilma, c'mere," she said to one of the girls.

Wilma tossed her hips as she crossed the room, thinking she had been chosen by one of the men. She was a wispy blonde, bland of face, modest of figure, as Szczygiel had noticed when she showed herself to him. She grinned at the two men, but her face fell when Bess shoved the picture toward her.

"Is that Claudia? Or is it not Claudia?" Bess asked.

Wilma covered her mouth with a hand. "Oooh-ugh! Jeez Christ! Yes, it's Claudia. An' she's *dead!*"

"I hadn't seen her for a long time," said Bess. "Five, six months. She was living with some guy."

"Do you know his name?"

Bess glanced at Wilma. "Yeah. Duroc. Paul Duroc. Right, Wilma?"

Wilma nodded.

"What did she call herself?" asked Szczygiel. "I mean her last name."

"We never called her anything but Claudia," said Bess. "I think she said her last name was Jordan, but we never paid much attention, because none of us ever use our real names."

"That's what she was called in Washington," said Wilma.

"Where was she from?"

Bess and Wilma shook their heads.

"Did she have a southern accent?"

The two women exchanged glances, then shook their heads again. "Not particularly," said Wilma. "Everybody in Washington does, but— She didn't any more than I do."

"How do you know she—"

Kennelly was interrupted by the sound of the doorbell. Bess went out and returned in a moment with a man. As soon as he saw there were two other men in the room, he turned his back to them. Wilma walked around him and exposed herself to him, as the other girl was doing. He chose the other girl. Bess took his money, and the girl left the room with him.

"How do you know the name Paul Duroc?" Kennelly asked.

"I lived with him myself for a couple weeks," said Wilma. "Till he got tired of me. It was kind of a vacation, you might say, for a couple weeks. He paid good. But it was boring."

"Where did you live with him?"

She mentioned the address and described the house. "He had the money to do things the way he wanted," she said. "He bought me perfume. I guess he thought girls smell."

"You know he's dead, too."

Wilma nodded. "I saw it in the paper." She shrugged. "Somebody was bound to get him, sooner or later."

"Why do you say that?"

"A lot of guys didn't like him. He carried a gun."

"Tell me about Claudia Jordan."

"There's not much to tell," said Bess. "Smart girl, knew what she wanted. She never was a regular here. She moved in, made a little money, moved on. I mean"—she paused, glanced at Wilma, then went on—"she wasn't the kind of girl you usually find in this business. I'll tell you, I always wondered something. Why'd she work for me? She could have worked for . . . well, for Blanche. I'm small, compared. She couldn't make the money here."

"I worked for Blanche, a little while," said Wilma. "Gotta be honest. The competition was too much. I didn't get picked often enough. Here . . . I get my share. A good share of less is better than a bad share of more."

"Sit down, Wilma," said Kennelly. "I bet Bess would be glad for you to take a drink."

Bess nodded, and the young woman sat down. Szczygiel was developing a fatherly concern for Wilma. He thought he saw tragedy. He was no innocent; he knew why these girls chose this life; yet somehow he doubted this one really wanted it.

Kennelly joined Wilma in a drink of rye. "I guess you're no dummy, Wilma," he said.

The young woman shrugged. "Maybe. Maybe not."

"You lived with Duroc two weeks. Right? And you were bored. You had to stay in the house all day, while he went to work, and wait for him to come home again. Right?"

"Right. Boring."

"I bet you explored everything in his house."

Wilma smiled. "Good bet."

"But you didn't steal anything, of course."

"He'd of killed me."

"But you saw everything. You saw what bank he used."

She nodded. "Two banks. First National and Farmers and Mechanics."

"He wrote his checks on First National."

"Yeah. But I saw a statement from Farmers and Mechanics. They wanted their rent for a safe-deposit box. It was funny, too. The statement was sent to the right address, but the name on it was William Lindsay."

Kennelly and Szczygiel were at Farmers & Mechanics Bank when it opened.

"It is irregular, Lieutenant. You do understand, it is quite irregular."

The president of the bank, one Charles Ogden—a fussy, owlish-looking man, bald, with round black-rimmed eyeglasses—was visibly impressed with the credentials of a D.C. police detective and an agent of the Secret Service, but he was reluctant to allow even them to open a safe-deposit box.

"Mr. Ogden, I can get a court order," said Kennelly. "It will take me an hour or so, but I can get it. In the meantime, something damn distressing may happen. I have good reason to believe a man recently murdered had a safe-deposit box in your bank. I have good reason to believe that the reason for his death remains in that box. I also have good reason to believe the men who killed him are looking for the box and will show up . . . with a key. I have good reason to believe another person was killed for that key. Now, you can cooperate or not—"

"Oh, I mean to cooperate, Lieutenant. You know—"

"We also have a key," said Kennelly. "We have a name. What we don't have is the box number. I propose to open the box in your presence, or in the presence of two men from the bank, if you'd prefer. We'll take nothing out. I just want to see what's in there."

Ogden led them back to the vault and introduced them to the deposit box attendant, a heavy, dark-haired woman named Florence Hennis. She had a notebook with the names and numbers.

"Paul Duroc," said Kennelly.

Miss Hennis opened her notebook to the D page and scanned the lines with her finger. She shook her head. "No. No one named Duroc."

"William Lindsay."

"Yes. A Mr. William Lindsay had a box, but he gave it up last November."

"Damn."

"Claudia Jordan," said Szczygiel.

Miss Hennis checked the Js and again shook her head.

"Elaine Curtis," said Szczygiel.

The C page. "Yessir. Elaine Curtis. I'll get the card."

"She couldn't have come in here and signed the name Paul Duroc," Szczygiel said to Kennelly. "If she opened the box, it had to be in her name. Her signature had to be on the card."

Miss Hennis showed them a file card. It was signed at the top, and the five signatures below matched the one at the top.

"Rented in November," she said. "It's been opened five times. Most recently on Monday. Also last Thursday."

"All right. We want to open it now."

"Uh— Mr. Ogden?"

The banker nodded. "It's all right. Police business."

Miss Hennis took the key, also her own key, and went into the vault to get the box. In a moment she returned, carrying a steel box. It was not one of the small boxes. This one was about twelve inches square and eight inches deep. She put it down on a table.

Kennelly opened it. The box was stuffed with cash: fifty-dollar bills, hundred-dollar bills, in bundles with rubber bands.

"I'm sorry about this, Mr. Ogden," said Szczygiel, "but we're going to have to count it. If we all four work on it, it shouldn't take too long."

It took ten minutes. When they were finished and added up the numbers from each of the bundles, the total was $54,300.

"I'm going to ask for more cooperation, Mr. Ogden, Miss Hennis," said Kennelly. "I'll get a court order about what we do with the money eventually. Right now it is evidence in two murders. I strongly suspect someone will come and try to take it."

"What should we do?" asked Ogden.

"Well . . ." said Kennelly. He turned to Miss Hennis. "Would you recognize Elaine Curtis if you saw her?"

"I'm not sure. Since I saw her twice in a few days, I might. On the other hand, lots of people come in . . ."

"Well, you won't see her. She's dead. But I expect a woman will come in here and call herself Elaine Curtis. She'll have a key. The signature won't match exactly, but don't worry about that. Delay her as much as you can, but let her have the box. Call the police. We'll have someone here before she can leave. Don't endanger yourself. Treat her as if you had no problem about her opening the box. Don't try to stop her, even if you don't see an officer around. Let her take the money and leave. We'll be someplace around, and we'll follow her."

Miss Florence Hennis nodded. "I will do exactly as you say."

"Fifty-four thousand dollars," said Mrs. Roosevelt thoughtfully. "Mr. Duroc—" She shook her head.

"Was no petty thief," said Szczygiel.

"And the Jane Doe—Claudia Jordan, Elaine Curtis, whoever she was—was a prostitute!"

"Yes. Part-time, anyway," said Kennelly.

They were again meeting in her study on the second floor of the White House, and as usual the First Lady had ordered coffee. She had just returned from riding in Rock Creek Park and had not changed out of her riding habit. She was wearing a white shirt and dark-brown necktie, a camel jacket, khaki jodhpurs, and high riding boots.

Stan Szczygiel would remark to Kennelly later that Mrs. Roosevelt had looked unusually handsome this morning, to which comment Kennelly would reply she could always look handsome if she didn't have such pitiful taste about her clothes.

"We may be certain of something, I believe, gentlemen," said the First Lady. "We still don't know who Jane Doe was. She was not Elaine Curtis, and she was not Claudia Jordan."

"Maybe Claudia Jordan," said Kennelly.

"No, I think not, actually," said Mrs. Roosevelt. "Let me review some of the facts you have given me this morning. You say she was affiliated from time to time with a house of prostitution. Is that not correct?"

"Yes."

"You also said it was not one of the city's better houses, did you not?"

Kennelly nodded. He was uncomfortable discussing this subject with Mrs. Roosevelt.

"I have looked at the photograph of her dead body. Only her face. You have examined her more thoroughly, haven't you, Lieutenant Kennelly? So, tell me— Was Jane Doe more attractive or less attractive than the young woman typically found associated with such establishments?"

Kennelly glanced at Szczygiel. "More attractive than the average, Ma'am. If I'm any judge."

"Why then do you suppose she was working in a small-time establishment? Is it not true that she would have made more money in a high-class establishment? If she were unusually attractive for a girl in that kind of work, why wasn't she working at the city's *best* establishment?"

"Mrs. Roosevelt, I couldn't guess."

"I can," she said. "And it *is* a guess. She was compelled, by force of circumstances, to work where she would be less conspicuous, where she was less likely to be seen by someone who might recognize her."

"Fugitive from justice?" Kennelly asked.

"Fugitive from justice, fugitive from a husband, fugitive from her family, fugitive from fellow criminals . . . but in any event a young woman compelled to earn a living for herself and do it where whomever she was hiding from was unlikely to find her."

"I imagine you're right," said Kennelly. "But where does it get us?"

"I will guess again," said the First Lady. "I will guess that she already knew Paul Duroc. I will guess that they were confederates in some scheme that has been in existence for a long time."

"On what basis do you make that guess?"

"Shortly after she moved into Mr. Duroc's house, he surrendered his safe-deposit box and put all that money in one that she had rented. Why would he do that?"

"To put another layer of secrecy over his stash," said Szczygiel.

"I agree. But notice— He trusted her. He gave her access to fifty-four thousand dollars."

"More than that," said Szczygiel. "She went to the box the day after he died and again on Monday. We can only guess how much she took out."

"Living in the Mayflower Hotel. Buying a fur coat and other fine clothes," said Mrs. Roosevelt. "I guess again. I guess she was preparing to unload the box completely and leave Washington."

"But somebody caught up with her," said Kennelly. "And killed her. And took her room key, went to her room, and found the safe-deposit box key."

"And you needn't, I think, worry about that somebody going to the Farmers and Mechanics Bank and trying to get into the box. I'm afraid your trap won't spring, Lieutenant."

"Why not?"

"You and Mr. Szczygiel had the other key for a week before you learned, quite by coincidence, what bank it was for. Very likely, the culprits have the same problem."

Kennelly's lips fluttered as he blew a loud sigh. "Which leaves us up the same damned creek, if you'll forgive me."

"No. You've done very good work. I suggest again you return your focus to the question of how the potassium cyanide got into Mr. Duroc's whiskey. And if you don't mind, I'm going to make another suggestion."

Kennelly nodded. "Glad to have a suggestion."

"Have the bank remove all the money from the box. While it is true that you might be able to follow whoever opens the box, it is also true you might lose the trail, if the person is clever, and it is also true that the person you follow might not know who all the culprits are and where they are to be found. But suppose they find the right bank, open the box, and it is empty."

Kennelly grinned. "Gotcha," he said. "Troubles and problems."

"They have committed two murders to gain access to that box," said Mrs. Roosevelt. "If they finally do gain access and find it empty—"

Szczygiel clapped his hands together. "By damn!" He laughed.

X

Mrs. Roosevelt left the White House late in the morning and had herself driven to Bethesda Naval Hospital for a visit with Louis McHenry Howe.

Howe, always an emaciated gnome of a man, was only a wraith now. He was dying of his Sweet Caporals, the cigarettes he had chain-smoked for forty years. His ravaged lungs could no longer support even his little body. The President said he had never had a better friend, and the First Lady—who years ago had disapproved of Howe but had changed her mind completely—agreed that she had never had a better friend either.

Louis McHenry Howe had been a capitol reporter in Albany when Franklin D. Roosevelt came there as a state senator. Howe had attached himself to the attractive young Democratic politician and in time had become indispensable. When the future President went to Washington as Assistant Secretary of the Navy under President Wilson, Howe had gone along as administrative assistant. He had labored on the 1920 vice-presidential campaign. He had hovered in the background, constantly encouraging and talking of a bright future, when Franklin Roosevelt lay stricken with polio, knowing he would never again walk, yet never giving up hope. Howe had planned the big campaigns: for governor of New York in 1928 and for President in 1932. As he lay dying in the hospital, in his restless mind he was planning the campaign of 1936.

Somehow over the years he had also found time to inculcate in Eleanor Roosevelt first a little knowledge of politics, then a little more, and in the end as finely honed an instinct for the electoral process as Franklin Roosevelt himself had. He had done it for her husband, probably more than for her, because he wanted a candidate's wife who would not be an impediment; still, he had done it for her, too. She owed a great debt to the little man with the hacking cough, and she tried to acknowledge it.

"Franklin will come, probably this weekend," she told Howe.

"No, no. He needn't. I know how difficult it is for him. He can telephone."

She was shocked by the visible deterioration in Howe's condition and had to guess he didn't have much longer. "Louis," she said, "you do look improved."

It was a little fiction they maintained, and he said, "I am better. I'll be out of here before long, certainly in time to get things going for this year."

"Will he be reelected, Louis?" she asked earnestly. His was the best judgment she could get. "It isn't certain, is it?"

"Nothing is certain, nothing in this world," said Howe. His voice was weak, and she had to draw her chair close to his bed to hear him. "But I'd make book on this one."

"Some of the reporting and editorializing is vicious," she said. "Even Franklin is hurt by some of the personal attacks. Louis, there is actually a story in circulation to the effect that Franklin was not crippled by infantile paralysis but by syphilis. Not only that, he is said to have been infected with it by *me*, and I am said to have acquired it by having had a connection with a Negro man."

"I've heard worse things than that," said Howe quietly, somberly, shaking his head. "That kind of talk is hateful, but it hurts only personally, not politically."

"Al Smith is taking the lead in organizing a cabal against Franklin."

"Tell Jim Farley to buy Al. We can outbid the boys who have him in their pockets. Poor Al. He's a pitiable man, you know."

"Who will the Republicans run?" she asked.

"Senator Borah, if they've got any sense. But they won't nominate a progressive. They'd rather lose. Which they will."

"You are satisfied now there will be no third party?"

Howe nodded. "Huey Long was the only man who could have started a third party that had any chance of drawing off enough votes to hurt Frank in 1936. The Communists don't amount to anything. The fascists . . ." He shook his head.

"What about Governor Landon?"

Again, Howe shook his head. "The only thing that can hurt Frank is overconfidence. He's got to get out and campaign. Tell him to go out and campaign."

Szczygiel and Kennelly caught up with Daniel Selmer as he was moving files from drawers into shipping cartons in his

office in the Senate Office Building. The suite consisted of
two small rooms, one for a secretary-receptionist and one
for the senatorial aide. Photographs of Senator Huey Long
still hung on the walls in both rooms.

Daniel Selmer was a young man—Szczygiel guessed he
was not yet thirty-five—so his baldness was premature. His
remaining hair was black, his eyes were small and brown
and conveyed, perhaps wrongly, an attitude of hostility and
suspicion.

He tossed another folder into a carton, then gave up on
the work and sat down behind his small yellow-oak desk. "I
guess it's not indecent of them to be pushing me out," he
said. "After all, the senator has been dead six months.
That's difficult for me to believe, but I suppose it's not
difficult for anyone else."

They were surprised that this Louisianan had not a trace
of southern accent.

"So. A D.C. detective and a Secret Service agent. Investigating the murder of Paul Duroc, I suppose."

"You were in the West Wing at the time," said Kennelly.

"No. I'd *been* in, stopped in to say good-bye to Dave
Oglesby. But that was—what?—two hours or more before
Duroc drank the poison."

"Did you get in to see Oglesby as soon as you arrived?"
asked Szczygiel.

"No, I had to wait a while. Maybe half an hour."

"Where did you wait?"

"In the second-floor lobby."

"Did you leave the lobby at any time?"

"Yes, I got up and went to the men's room."

"Which is just across the hall from Paul Duroc's office,"
said Szczygiel.

Selmer grinned and nodded. "Right. So I could have popped into Duroc's office and put poison in his whiskey. Except for one little thing."

"What's that?"

"Duroc was sitting there at his desk."

"Did you stop in and say hello?"

"Of course not!"

"Why not?"

"Because that son of a bitch had stolen the campaign fund, that's why not. Huey's money. And when we demanded it, he laughed at us. He said there wasn't any money; Huey'd taken it. He said Huey'd had no intention of running for President and had been using the idea that he was just as a way of raking in cash."

"You're glad he's dead," said Kennelly. "You'd have liked to kill him yourself."

Selmer nodded. "I won't deny that. But I didn't do it. I didn't have a chance to poison his whiskey. He was sitting right there at his desk."

"We have your word on that but no other evidence," said Kennelly.

"I believe it's still American law, Lieutenant, that you have to prove your case, not that I have to prove my innocence."

"I've got motive and opportunity, Mr. Selmer," said Kennelly. "Now, I'm going to ask for your cooperation in something. I'd like to have a photograph of you. I want to show it to a few people. If you don't want to give me a photo, I can take you downtown and let the police mug-shot photographer take one for me."

"I don't have a picture of me," said Selmer. "Tell you what I'll do. I'll come in with you voluntarily, so you can have your man take my picture. Show you what a good guy I am.''

They agreed to that, and Selmer shrugged into his overcoat, put on his hat, and went with Kennelly and Szczygiel to the police car. On the way to headquarters, Szczygiel asked Selmer about Thérèse Rolland.

"Huey favored her," said Selmer. "Something about her intrigued him. I don't know if it was her looks or her personality or what."

"Somebody told us he'd seen her dancing in her underwear," said Kennelly.

Selmer nodded. "Couple times. I mean, I saw her do it a couple times. Terry drinks a lot. Maybe you know that. It used to amuse Huey to get her drunk and see what stupid things she'd do. We had private parties, y' know. For selected guys. One night Terry got up on a table, took off everything but her panties and a brassiere, and claimed she was dancing like they do in France. You know the old song the boys brought back in 1919: 'In the southern part of France, the women wear no pants, and the dance they do—' You know. The boys kept telling her she wasn't dancing right unless she took off her pants, but she wouldn't do it. Huey thought it was hilarious. He got her to do it again, one time that I saw and maybe other times. Something else she wouldn't do was . . . Well, she wouldn't go to a room with a man."

"Did Huey ask her to do that?"

Selmer shook his head grimly. "No. Duroc. After Huey died, Duroc laid claim to Terry. Not for himself, really, I don't think. But as an . . . asset, to use to promote his fortunes. She's known around town. A lot of guys are intrigued by her. Nobody'd want to be married to her. She

could have been helpful to Duroc, some ways. I don't know
what he thought he was going to do. Run for Congress.
Become a big lobbyist. He was limitlessly ambitious. Huey
worried about that."

"You're telling us that Terry had reason to hate Duroc."

"Everybody who knew him had reason to hate Duroc."

At headquarters they had Daniel Selmer photographed,
then had a uniformed officer return him to the Senate Office
Building. While he was at headquarters, Kennelly showed
him the picture of Jane Doe. Selmer said he'd never seen
her.

Mrs. Roosevelt volunteered to inquire of Ernest McSweeney
herself. She had spotted his name on the guest list for a
luncheon she was attending at the Raleigh Hotel. The luncheon was sponsored by a group of state commissioners of
agriculture of southern states, and would be addressed by
Secretary of Agriculture Henry A. Wallace. The First Lady
would be introduced but would not speak.

Since the topic before the meeting was the state of the
South's agricultural economy, it was not unlikely that the
lobbyist for the sugar industry was picking up the tab for
the luncheon. Indeed, when she saw McSweeney, whom she
had met several times before, his manner as he moved from
one handshake to another was that of a man who was
paying for the luncheon.

A man with abundant white hair and a flushed face, he
needed only mustache and goatee to make him the epitome
of a southern plantation owner: a colonel of state militia.
Though he was wearing a handsome double-breasted gray
wool suit, she had seen him in white linen in the summer.

Winter or summer, he wore a fresh red carnation in his lapel.

They were not seated together, or near each other, and she had to watch for an opportunity to talk to him. It did not come until after Henry Wallace had made his speech.

"Mr. McSweeney, I wanted to talk with you. Could I offer you a ride to your office?"

"I should be happy, gracious lady, to create any sort of opportunity for us to talk."

The distance from the Raleigh Hotel to the White House was not far enough to give them time to talk, so she asked the Secret Service agent—who happened to be Dominic Deconcini—and the driver to wait outside the car on the driveway at the South Portico while she talked to the lobbyist.

"I am sure you are aware that Mr. Paul Duroc was murdered in the Executive Wing last Wednesday," she said.

McSweeney nodded. "I am, of course."

"Yes. Well, the murder remains unsolved. We are reduced to such farfetched procedures as inquiring of everyone shown by the diaries to have been in the Executive Wing that afternoon."

" 'We' are reduced to so doing? Do I understand that you are taking part in the investigation, my dear lady?"

"I am offering some advice and assistance. It is a rather delicate matter to inquire of such people as yourself, and it does seem better that I ask you a question or two than it be done by a somewhat gruff District police detective."

"That is thoughtful of you," said Ernest McSweeney. His hands, in gray suede gloves, rested on his ebony walking stick. "So what questions may I answer?"

"You were in the Executive Wing late in the afternoon

when Mr. Duroc died, waiting to see Vice President Garner. You were observed walking around on the first and second floors, speaking to the many people you know. It is has been suggested that you could have stopped into Mr. Duroc's office and put the poison in—"

"In what, my dear, gracious lady?" asked McSweeney. "I have been told that Miss Rolland drank from the same bottle of bourbon. The cyanide was necessarily, therefore, introduced into his glass, just before he drank from it. And that could have been done only by Miss Rolland. I am afraid the case against that unfortunate young lady is, as they say in police work, airtight."

"Then assist me, if you can, in determining why a young woman, as yet unidentified, who lived with Mr. Duroc was shot to death on the street night before last. Assist me even in identifying her."

Ernest McSweeney looked out the window at the driver and the Secret Service agent standing uncomfortably in the grass by the driveway in the cold wind of a March day. "Mrs. Roosevelt," he said soberly, "you have to understand that there are three Washingtons at least. One is the world you and your husband live in: of honest dedicated people trying to govern the country. One is the world of politicians and lobbyists, venal in varying degrees, interested in earning a living. Still another is a world of criminals. Criminals, my very dear lady. Paul Duroc was of *that* world."

"Where did Senator Long stand?" she asked.

"Astride them all, I suppose," said McSweeney. "There was an idealistic streak in Huey. And an ambitious, selfish streak. And a vicious criminal streak. They say the same of Arthur Flegenheimer—Dutch Schultz—in New York, though of course in a different milieu."

"What did Paul Duroc do that made him a criminal? I've heard he stole the Long campaign fund, or part of it, but was there anything more?"

"As a government auditor, he chose his targets for his own advantage. He took payments to stand aside, payments to conceal his findings. The watchdog, dear lady, was stealing from the house he was supposed to be watching."

"And did some proficient work to cover himself," she said.

"Exactly."

"Would you consent to look at the photograph of the young woman found dead on the street yesterday morning?"

"Of course."

"One thing more, Mr. McSweeney," said Mrs. Roosevelt. "Did Paul Duroc ever steal from *you*?"

McSweeney smiled and nodded. "In a sense. But not directly. As lobbyist for a southern interest, I kept my peace with Huey Long, when he was governor as well as when he was senator. When Huey died, Paul Duroc looted Huey's war chest. I suspect he was preparing to leave the country. There would have been enough money there for him to do it. It is rather annoying, don't you think, to know that money you have contributed to buy a politician's goodwill has been stolen by one of his aides?"

Mrs. Roosevelt nodded. "I should think that would be most annoying."

"It could have been Congressman Devol or Commander Sykes, too," the First Lady said to Szczygiel and Kennelly. "They were in his office that afternoon. Why were they there? To pay him for quieting his findings about the contract to build the seaplane ramp at Pensacola? Was he blackmailing them? There would be little point in asking them, I suppose. They would deny they poisoned Mr. Duroc and then fall back on the same answer: that only Miss Rolland could have introduced the poison into his drink."

"So we're back to that," said Kennelly. "She was the only one who could have done it."

"Unless someone very cleverly—what is the term— 'framed' her," said Mrs. Roosevelt.

"Can you think of any way it could have been done?" asked Szczygiel.

"I shall keep the idea to myself. That way the two of you will continue to explore possibilities."

"It would help if we knew where the potassium cyanide came from," said Kennelly.

"It would help if we knew who Jane Doe was," said Mrs. Roosevelt.

Alfred Schmidt peered up over the gold frames of his spectacles. "So, Lieutenant Kennelly," he said. "You have more dirty jewelry for me to clean *gratis*?"

"No, Uncle," said Kennelly. "I've got some pictures for you to look at."

"Not dirty pictures. I'm an old man."

"Not dirty pictures, Uncle," said Kennelly with a wide grin. "Pictures of dirty people maybe."

"Worse! Who are these dirty people?"

"You tell me," said Kennelly.

He showed him a picture of Thérèse Rolland, and the old man shook his head and said he'd never seen her.

He showed him a picture of Jane Doe. Alfred Schmidt squinted over that photograph for a moment, then began to nod. "Dead, hmm? Yes. I've seen her. Look here." He turned to the big iron safe behind his counter, opened a small drawer, and pulled out a box. From the box he lifted a diamond ring attached by a tag to a string. "Uh-huh. There you are."

The ring was of white gold, with a large diamond. Kennelly turned it over and over, but he found no engraving on it, not even an initial.

"Carat and a half," said the pawnbroker. "Nicely cut, nicely set. I let her have two hundred dollars on it—meaning it's worth . . . seven hundred."

Kennelly read the tag. "Claudia Jordan" had pawned the ring in August 1935. She had given a Georgetown address: the street address for Bess's bawdy house.

"This was the second time she pawned it," said Schmidt. "Earlier, in like maybe February last year, she pawned it and then came back and redeemed it. I didn't try to sell it. I figured for sure she'd come back. Now . . . You're not going to tell me it's evidence?"

"You satisfied it's not stolen?" Kennelly asked.

"No, I'm not satisfied it's not stolen. But the cops have looked at it twice, an insurance adjuster once, and nobody has claimed it's stolen. It's not on anybody's list."

"So she was in here, what, three times? Pawn, redeem, and pawn again. Did you clean it for her? Could she have known where you kept your cyanide?"

Schmidt shook his head.

"A diamond ring worth seven hundred dollars," Kennelly mused. "She was so short of money she pawned it for two hundred. She worked as a prostitute sometimes, Uncle. So she got money and she came and got her ring back. And a few months later she pawns it again."

"Story of the pawn brokerage business, Kennelly. I don't make loans to the chronically poor. They never have anything to pawn. It's people with seesaw fortunes who pawn their possessions to get cash."

"Also thieves," said Kennelly.

"I should deny it? I cooperate with the police. I couldn't stay in business if I didn't. There are just three pawnshops in Washington. All of us cooperate with the police."

Kennelly showed him the picture of Daniel Selmer. Schmidt shook his head.

"I had a call from Farmers and Mechanics Bank," said Kennelly to Mrs. Roosevelt and Szczygiel. "Nothing. No one has come in."

Mrs. Roosevelt smiled. *"They* don't know where to take their key either, to what bank," she said. "If someone killed Jane Doe to get the key, they made a big mistake. They should have followed her. Sooner or later, she would have led them to the right bank."

Kennelly sighed loudly. "Terry Rolland killed Paul Duroc," he said. "She didn't do it too damn smart, either. It *might* have been smart, but she did it so nobody else could have done it. Then somebody killed Jane Doe. They didn't do that too damn smart either. Like you said, Ma'am, if they killed her for the deposit box key, they made a big mistake. What we're dealing with is politician crooks, not professional criminals."

"Are professional criminals so smart, Lieutenant?" asked Mrs. Roosevelt.

"Well . . . You've got a point there. The truth is, Sherlock Holmes was never needed. There was never a crook smart enough to need a Sherlock Holmes to catch him."

"Oh, I suspect that is not exactly true, Lieutenant," said the First Lady.

"No. No, you're right. But they're rare. Smart crooks are rare. The whole business of writing mystery novels is based on a wrong idea, which is that criminals are so smart it takes great cleverness to catch them. The typical one leaves the clues laying all over. I said no smart crook would ever be caught because he left his fingerprints. I believe that. Still, we do get them that way sometimes. Which means they weren't smart crooks."

"Oh, Lieutenant Kennelly, you are destroying the premise underlying a highly entertaining minor fiction genre!"

"Sorry, Ma'am," said Kennelly with a broad grin. "I'm just your everyday professional cop, laboring in the vineyard. I'm in touch with criminals every day, and cops, too. I still haven't run across a genius. And, J. Edgar Loverboy to the contrary, I've never seen an FBI agent yet who could find his way to the bathroom. What was it Edison is supposed to have said about invention? That it was one percent inspiration and ninety-nine percent perspiration? You know, if you think about it, Sherlock Holmes solved his crimes, really, by hard damned work. Watson was always complaining that Holmes wouldn't stop to rest. It wasn't his insights so much as his hard work that made him a genius. Well . . . Excuse me, I guess I've made a speech."

"And a very good one, Lieutenant," said Mrs. Roosevelt. "Our murderers have made at least one mistake that we know about: failing to realize the name of the bank would not be stamped on the deposit box key. Let us look for other mistakes. I am sure there have been some."

"Well, I wish we could lay our fingers on the big one," said Kennelly.

*   *   *

The President asked Missy to take some dictation in his study between the cocktail hour and dinner. He told her when they were finished that she should send that down to the West Wing, where someone would be on duty to type it, so he could sign the dictated letters first thing in the morning. He was in a jovial mood and said—

"If you can come down to dinner, I have something funny to tell you,"

If she were coming down to dinner was a jovial way to speak. *Of course* she was coming down to dinner. Very few evenings, when he did not leave the White House for some sort of function, did they have dinner otherwise than in his bedroom, from trays brought up from the kitchen. The First Lady was welcome to join them but never did. They would have dinner as usual, listen to some music, and talk.

Apart maybe from Louis Howe, who was tragically and prematurely dying, Missy LeHand was probably Franklin D. Roosevelt's best friend.

Louis was his best political and personal friend. Missy was his best personal friend. Like any politician, he had a wide circle of friends, including many in whom he could confide. Louis and Missy were the only ones who knew the anguish of his life, knew it intimately, had seen his tears. And now, Missy alone would know.

Tonight he was jovial. For one reason, they would share a bottle of wine sent by Blackjack Endicott. It would enliven even the determinedly bland cooking that came up from the White House kitchen.

"It's odd," he said when their trays were before them. She sat on the left side of the bed, tray beside her; he sat propped up against pillows, tray on his lap. "We have inadequate intelligence about anything going on in the world. If the Japanese navy were lying off San Francisco, about to bombard, we wouldn't know it. Not necessarily. But when it comes to petty gossip, we seem to know everything."

Missy laughed. "It's more interesting, anyway."

"All right. This is what I hear. Edward Albert Christian George Andrew Patrick David—"

"Effdee," she interrupted, "why does the poor man have so many names?"

The President took a sip of wine, savored it, and then explained. "Okay. It's Edward because his grandfather was Edward: King Edward the Seventh. Albert because his great-grandfather was Prince Albert—and an heir to the throne born while old Victoria was still alive was damned well going to be named Albert. Christian was his other grandfather's name: the father of Queen Alexandra. He was King of Denmark, you know. George is a veddy, veddy *English* name. Got to get that in. Besides, his father was George the Fifth. Andrew is a Scots name. Got to keep the Scots happy. Then Patrick is Irish and David is Welsh. If they took India entirely seriously, he'd probably also be Mohandas or something."

Missy laughed. "If they'd won the Hundred Years War, he'd also have to be Louis or Pierre."

"Right," said the President. "Anyway, the gossip coming in from London is that he is absolutely stricken with an American woman by the name of Wallis Warfield Simpson. Can't live without her. The story is that her English husband, Simpson, with stiff upper lip and all that, is going to divorce this woman so his king can have her."

"A romance," said Missy with a grin.

"Except for one little thing," said the President. "British Intelligence has a fat dossier on this woman. Among the items in that file is the alleged fact that she served an apprenticeship in eroticism in a Shanghai bawdy house. The rumor is that only a woman with such training can arouse the difficult-to-stimulate King Edward the Eighth. And that is why—"

"Effdee! Stop!"

The President shrugged. "I only report what I hear from England. Access to items from the files of British Intelligence is one of the advantages of being President of the United States."

Missy pushed her tray aside and leaned over his, to kiss Franklin Roosevelt warmly. "Effdee . . ." she whispered. "You are a *devil*!"

His smile disappeared. "Would that I were," he said softly.

She repeated her kiss. "Devil enough, Boss," she murmured.

Stan Szczygiel left the White House a little after seven, dined alone at Harvey's, then drove to Georgetown. He arrived at Bess's house a little after nine.

"Well . . . Agent Szczygiel," said Bess as she welcomed him at the door. "What can I do for you tonight?"

"Unofficial visit," said Szczygiel awkwardly. "I'd like to see Wilma."

"Unofficially?"

"Right. I'd like to . . . visit her. You know."

"Oh, sure. She'll be honored. C'mon in. She's busy right now, but she'll be free in a few minutes."

Szczygiel sat down uneasily. Bess offered him a shot of whiskey, which he accepted.

"Still don't know who killed Claudia, I suppose."

"No. We don't even know who she really was."

"Let me tell you some things about her," said Bess. "They came to me after you guys left last night and I got to thinkin'. I said she wasn't one of us, not the kind of girl I usually get. Like, she never pronounced a word wrong, that I could tell. She spoke like a . . . lady. She sat like a lady, walked like a lady. She was no trash, that girl."

"Thanks," said Szczygiel.

After another minute he heard the front door close. Wilma had just said good-bye to her customer. She came into the waiting room.

"Look who's here to see ya," said Bess. "Unofficial. Wants a visit."

"Wants . . . two visits, let's say," said Szczygiel, handing Bess a ten-dollar bill. "Wants some extra time."

Bess grinned. "All the time you want, Stan."

In the tiny room upstairs, Szczygiel did what Wilma expected. She'd have thought him odd if he hadn't. And he enjoyed the experience. But he had come to talk with her.

"I'm going to ask you a flat-out question, Wilma," he said. "Would you like to get out of this business?"

The young woman picked up a package of Camels from the table by the bed. "I suppose any girl in this business would like to get out," she said as she struck a paper match and lit a cigarette.

"When you went to live with Duroc, you were bored," said Szczygiel.

"There was more to it than that," she said. "He was . . . rough."

"Are you saying he hurt you?"

"Yes. Don't ask for details."

"Well . . . Flat out. Would you like to come and live with me? I'm an old man. My wife has been dead a long time. I'm lonely."

Wilma drew deeply on her cigarette. "I've got to make a living," she said.

"Not if you live with me, you don't. I'll provide the house, the food, your clothes, and I'll give you some spending money. If you don't like it, you can always come back here. Bess'll take you. If you stay with me . . . Well, in a couple of years I'm going to retire. My idea is to move to Florida. How'd you like that?"

Wilma nodded. "I'll try it," she said quietly.

XI

"Is it useful to summarize?" asked Mrs. Roosevelt. "You know, I am given to summarization, usually written down. I find it clarifies things."

She had a chalkboard on a tripod and began to scrawl names and words, as Stan Szczygiel and Ed Kennelly watched.

First she wrote—

DUROC

MOTIVE	OPPORTUNITY
Terry Rolland: revenge for abuse. Maybe blackmail.	Ample, maybe only opportunity.
Daniel Selmer: revenge, maybe seeking to recover Long funds.	Possible, was in area, could have been in office.
Ernest McSweeney: same, emphasis on latter.	Possibility similar.

Other: Duroc widely disliked as cheat, thief, etc.	Anyone in West Wing second floor.

"JANE DOE"

MOTIVE	OPPORTUNITY
Access to safe-deposit box.	Anyone on street. *But must have known she would be there.*

"We haven't talked about what I've just written," said the First Lady. "The killer of Jane Doe must have found out she was living at the Mayflower Hotel."

"What was she doing out at that hour of the morning?" asked Szczygiel.

"Keeping an appointment, making a rendezvous. It has to be something like that," said Mrs. Roosevelt.

"She was hiding," said Kennelly. "Wasn't she?"

"I have a suggestion," said Mrs. Roosevelt. "Check with the passport office. Isn't it possible that Jane Doe was planning to leave the country? With more than fifty thousand dollars available to her, she may have been planning on hiding in some place very far away. South America . . . Asia."

"Not a bad idea, either," said Kennelly, "considering what happened to her."

"Let us indulge ourselves in a bit of speculation," said Mrs. Roosevelt. "To begin with, she was involved in some way in Paul Duroc's dishonest schemes. It's interesting—is it not?—that he trusted her enough to let her have a key to his safe-deposit box."

"But maybe he didn't, really," said Szczygiel. "Maybe he put the box in her name to make it even more difficult to find. He kept a key at home and a key at the office, so he could get to the box fast if he had to run."

"There is a small problem with that," said the First Lady. "Paul Duroc could not open the box, whether he had a key or not, because Jane Doe had to appear and sign the card—to sign it 'Elaine Curtis,' of course."

"Do you suppose she was a real confederate of his, not just a slavey?" Kennelly asked.

"We need to know," said Mrs. Roosevelt. "As I said, let us speculate. She learned of his death, probably the evening when it occurred. She had to leave the house quickly, assuming investigators would soon arrive."

"Or the murderer," said Szczygiel.

"Somebody," said Mrs. Roosevelt. "She gathered a few things—most importantly the safe-deposit key—and fled. Very likely she was on the streets all night, or sitting in a bus station or somewhere. The next morning she went to the bank and took some money from the box. That made it possible for her to check into the Mayflower Hotel. Now she has time to consider what she is going to do. Perhaps she decides she has to leave the country. Now, that is pure speculation, but it seems reasonable she would think of that, all things considered."

"I think it's a real possibility," said Kennelly.

"She could not appear at the passport office before Friday. Maybe not even that soon. She would have to obtain a birth certificate. She would need a photograph of herself. Maybe she didn't apply for her passport until Monday. Or Tuesday."

"And maybe not at all," said Szczygiel.

"Or maybe she already had one," said Kennelly.

"A simple check would give us the answer," said Mrs.

Roosevelt. "And think of it. If she had to show a birth certificate—"

When the two men had left, Mrs. Roosevelt sat and stared at her chart for a few minutes, then rose and scribbled some more. Under the "JANE DOE" heading, she amended the first entry under motive and then continued—

MOTIVE	OPPORTUNITY
Access to safe-deposit box: *all.*	Anyone on street. *But must have known she would be there*
Terry Roland: ?	None, in jail.
Selmer, McSweeney: same, access.	Possible.
Person(s) hired. Their fee.	Would have made their opportunity.

She sat down, then rose and added a line across the bottom—

All depends on identity of Jane Doe.

"She was very quick," said Florence Hennis. "I delayed her as much as I could without making myself obvious—which is what you told me to do. She was in here and out of here in three minutes."

Ed Kennelly looked at the signature on the card. "She wasn't very good at copying the signature," he said. "Her 'Elaine Curtis' isn't very much like the other signatures."

"Right," agreed Florence Hennis. "But she had the key. I

didn't question the signature. You told me not to. I brought out the box. She took it in a cubicle and opened it. In ten seconds she came out, handed me the key, and said she was finished. By then I had sent out the word to call the police. I took as much time as I could about putting the box back in its slot in the vault, but when I came back and handed her the key the police still had not arrived."

"So she left," said Kennelly.

"I watched as much as I could. A man was waiting for her in the lobby of the bank. Both of them were shaking their heads hard as they left. I knew why. She'd told him the box was empty."

"Good. Now— Tell me what she looked like."

Florence Hennis kept rubbing her hands together, as if she were scrubbing them. It was the only sign she gave that her experience with the imposter Elaine Curtis had unnerved her. "Well . . ." she said. "You'd told me Elaine Curtis is dead. Except for that, I might possibly have taken this girl for the same one. She looked something like her. The same type, same build, same coloration. On the other hand— Something. I don't know. The original one was prettier."

"How was she dressed?"

"Ordinary. Very ordinary. Brown coat. Little feathered hat, also brown. Of course she was carrying a valise. She expected to carry away fifty thousand dollars in cash."

"Wearing gloves? No fingerprints?"

"Tan suede."

"Was she nervous?" Kennelly asked.

"I'd say tense. Right. More like tense," said Florence Hennis. "She had control of herself."

"Would you recognize her if I brought in a picture of her?"
"Probably."

The President left the White House at noon, on his way to a luncheon he had been looking forward to. He did not often leave the White House for luncheons, but today he made an exception. A group of American cartoonists had conceived a project of creating a museum of cartoon art, and President Roosevelt had gladly agreed to lend his presence to the luncheon that would kick off a campaign to raise the needed funds.

The President was of course the featured speaker. What he planned to do was read some cartoon strips. Farley had put together a folio of them; and, arriving at the luncheon early, had identified the cartoonists present and put their strips on top. Knowing that *Barney Google* was one of the President's favorites, he had put it first, and during the lunch he brought Billy DeBeck, the artist, forward to shake the President's hand and say hello.

He brought Harold Gray forward for another reason. The creator of *Little Orphan Annie* was degenerating into a paranoid superpatriot apologist for big business—his Daddy Warbucks was a billionaire munitions magnate—and Farley hoped that meeting the President and seeing him as a warm and friendly man might temper Gray a little and discourage him from using *Annie* for vitriolic attacks on the New Deal. Nothing of the kind was spoken. The President said he followed the adventures of Annie and was pleased to meet Gray. Gray said he was honored to meet the President.

When the meal was finished, Farley helped the President to stand.

"I am pleased," he said, "to meet with a group of men who, on the whole, as I am convinced, have a more realistic view of the world than any of us politicians. It is good, too, to meet with a group of men who always meet their deadlines. I would like to send you up to Capitol Hill, to see if you could teach that virtue to the Congress."

After a few more remarks, he began to read cartoon strips, doing the dialogue in assorted accents and describing the action—

"Well, here we have Barney Google, astride his steed Sparkplug, racing as fast as he can. His faithful groom Sunshine races alongside, astride the ostrich, Rudy. Sunshine says, 'Boss, wot's de idea o' makin' me get outa mah bed dis early in the morning fo'?' And Google says, 'Very simple, Sunshine. We are broke and can't pay our hotel bill, and the clerk said if I didn't settle up today I'd have the sheriff on my trail.' In the second panel the sheriff on his motorcycle appears in the background, shouting 'Halt! In the name of the law!' 'Giddy-ap, Sparkplug!' says Google. In the third panel, Sparkplug dashes across the state line. 'Foiled!' complains the sheriff. 'Whoa, Sparky,' says Google."

The President laughed heartily, as did his audience: three hundred artists, publishers, editors, politicians. The President called on Billy DeBeck to stand and take a bow.

Next he read a strip in which the lovable moocher Wimpy told Popeye, "My friend, I am famished. For the price of a hamburger, I would gladly mow your lawn—if you had a lawn to mow."

In another *Popeye* strip that was a particular favorite of the President's, Roughhouse, the keeper of the diner, asked Popeye, "Are the oysters good today, Popeye?" and Popeye replied, "Yaas, they is exter nice."

The President pointed to Elzie Segar, creator of *Popeye,* and the cartoonist stood grinning and bowed.

Next he read a strip from *Blondie* and called on Chic Young to stand.

Finally, he read a sequence from a new strip with which he was not familiar. It was called *Li'l Abner* and featured a hillbilly family with comic accents and mores.

Afterwards, Farley brought to the speaker's table the young cartoonist who created *Li'l Abner,* a Bostonian named Alfred G. Caplin, who signed his strips Al Capp. The young man struggled forward a little awkwardly, swinging a wooden leg. He faintly resembled his hero, Abner: having a strong square face, a cleft chin, and unruly black hair that persisted in falling over his forehead.

"Your strip is very inventive, Mr. Capp," said the President. "I'm going to start following it."

"Thank you, Mr. President. You can substitute Abner for Joe Palooka."

"Al used to draw the *Joe Palooka* strip for Ham Fisher," Farley explained.

"You mean Fisher doesn't draw it himself?" the President asked.

"No, he just hires some hungry young artist for peanuts, sits back and makes money, and lets the kid do the work," said Capp.

"Do I detect a note of bitterness?" the President asked with a chuckle.

"Sorry," Capp laughed. "I don't get much of anything political into *Abner,* Mr. President, but if ever I do, you can be sure it will say something admiring of you."

* * *

Lee Slusser, the detective assigned by Kennelly to check the records of McAllister Supply Company, had returned to the office of the company president.

"I've done everything I can think of to help you," the man said. His name was Weyrich; a young man who had inherited the company from his father, as he had explained to Slusser on Wednesday. "I've shown your photographs to all my clerks. We've run through the records for the past twelve months. You understand, we don't sell much potassium cyanide, and we pretty well know who our customers are. The stuff is very dangerous, you know, and we don't sell it to just anybody. Reviewing the sales over the past year, either I personally or one of my clerks could identify every purchaser."

"Nobody bought an unusually large amount?" Slusser asked.

"No, but a would-be murderer wouldn't have to. All he'd need is a pinch of it. He could lift it out of somebody's supply, and that somebody wouldn't even notice that it was gone. The limiting factor is that you have to know *how* to use it. I read the newspaper accounts of the death of this man Duroc. He was killed by somebody who knew how to use potassium cyanide. Otherwise, he might have writhed and retched for an hour."

Weyrich gave Slusser the list of every purchase of potassium cyanide since March 1935, and Slusser left.

Detective Lieutenant Ed Kennelly did something very unusual for him. He clamped the red flasher light to the top of his car, sounded his siren, and sped through Washington traffic. He had been in his office when the word came that

the keeper of a pawnshop on Fifteenth Street had been
killed in a robbery.

Alfred Schmidt.

Kennelly squatted beside the body of the elderly pawnbroker where it was sprawled behind his counter. He had
been shot several times, in the chest and throat.

The shop had been ransacked. The safe was open. Kennelly had no real idea what had been in there, but the boxes
had been pulled out and the contents scattered over the
counter.

He examined the assorted jewelry. The Jane Doe ring was
missing.

"It doesn't necessarily mean anything," he told Mrs. Roosevelt later. "It was maybe the most valuable item of jewelry
he had in pawn. A robber would naturally have taken it.
What was left was mostly junk. The robber or robbers may
have taken the best pieces and scrammed. Once they had
shot the old fellow, they didn't have time to hang around.
It's reasonable that they scooped up what was worth the
most money and took off."

"Is it just a coincidence, then, that the same pawnbroker
from whose shop a quantity of potassium cyanide was stolen also took the Jane Doe ring in pawn, and now has been
murdered and the ring stolen?"

"It may be a coincidence," said Kennelly, "that the one
pawnbroker in Washington who used potassium cyanide
was also the biggest pawnbroker in town and the one Jane
Doe went to see when she wanted to borrow money on her
ring. If I had ever wanted to pawn anything, I would have
gone to Schmidt's. The others in Washington are small-
timers."

"You say he was shot with a small-caliber weapon. So was Jane Doe."

Kennelly nodded. "The bullet wounds looked to me like they'd been made by a small-caliber pistol. The bullets are at the ballistics lab now. I expect a report within the hour."

"I'd appreciate it if you'd let me know the results of the ballistics tests," she said. "You can guess what I suspect."

"It's possible," said Kennelly.

At the passport office, Szczygiel confronted an indignant chief clerk, a sixty-year-old man with a flushed face and spectacles resting on his plump cheeks more than on his nose, who insisted the work of his office could not be disrupted by searching applications out of order.

"Really, Agent Szczygiel, we receive hundreds of applications. Going through them as you demand will get them all out of order. Besides, when we issue a passport, our file is closed on it."

"Mr. Lattin," said Szczygiel rigidly, "the Secret Service is investigating a murder, a possible threat to the safety of the President, and I don't care if you and your staff accomplish nothing more today than search through those applications. That is what you are going to do. That is how you are going to spend your time. If necessary, I will get a direct order from the Secretary of State."

"Will the White House accept responsibility for the fact that this office will run significantly behind in its processing of applications?" sniffed Lattin.

"Will you take responsibility if the man who killed Paul Duroc remains at large and later attempts to kill the President?" asked Szczygiel.

"*That* will not happen," said Lattin loftily.

"No," Szczygiel agreed. "We're not going to allow that to happen. So get crackin', buster. You have all day, but I don't."

A younger man, who had overheard all of the conversation, stepped up to the counter and spoke. "May I suggest something that might save a great deal of time?" he asked Lattin.

"*Anything* that will save a great deal of time," said Lattin.

"If this passport was applied for on Monday or Tuesday," said the young man, "it will have been processed by now and is waiting to be picked up. We have, Sir, only about a half dozen passports waiting to be picked up."

Lattin bestowed a scornful glance on the young man, as if he relished the confrontation with the agent and did not want it to end before he'd found all the satisfaction he could in it. "Very well," he sighed. "I suppose that's as good a place to start as any."

The third passport he showed Stan Szczygiel was for Jane Doe.

"I simply took the file from them and brought it here," Szczygiel said to Mrs. Roosevelt. "I think we know who Jane Doe was, at last."

The First Lady opened the file folder and examined, first, the application.

The applicant was Antonia Caroline Long, of Washington, giving a Georgetown address, born in Pierre Port, St. Martin Parish, Louisiana, on September 8, 1912, citizen of the United States by birth.

In support of her application the applicant had submitted a birth certificate—

CERTIFICATE OF LIVE BIRTH

Born this 8th day of September, 1912, a female, to be christened:

ANTONIA CAROLINE LONG

Child of: H. P. Long of Baton Rouge, East Baton Rouge Parish, 19 years of age, drummer; and Antonia Matilde Boudreau, spinster, of Pierre Port, St. Martin Parish, 17 years of age.

    I certify that I attended at said birth and that the above-named child was born alive.

                (Signed) Alice Farnsworth
                                 Midwife

"My lord!"

Szczygiel nodded. "Yeah. Huey Long started out in life as a baking powder salesman, traveling the back roads of Louisiana, in older parlance called a 'drummer.' 'H. P. Long.' It has to be him."

"And nineteen years old," said Mrs. Roosevelt. "That fits. That's how old he was in 1912."

"Born of 'Antonia Matilde Boudreau, *spinster.*' That means the little girl was illegitimate. Nice of them to put that on her birth certificate, wasn't it?"

"Customary, I'm afraid," said Mrs. Roosevelt.

"What a tangle of possibilities this creates!"

"I'm going to call Lieutenant Kennelly," said the First Lady. "He is coming back here shortly. I'm going to ask him to bring Miss Rolland with him."

After she telephoned Kennelly, Mrs. Roosevelt walked across to the West Wing for a moment's conversation with

Sandra Wilson. She wanted to ask her if she knew whether or not Duroc had possessed a current passport. But it was five-thirty, and Sandra Wilson had gone for the day.

On her way back to her study, the First Lady met Ed Kennelly leading Terry Rolland toward the elevator. Terry walked glumly, with her head down, wearing a lined and bulky denim jacket over her jail uniform. She was handcuffed.

In the study, Kennelly took off the handcuffs, and Terry shrugged out of the ugly jacket.

"Have you ever seen or heard of this?" the First Lady asked Terry as soon as she sat down, handing her the birth certificate of Antonia Caroline Long.

"Rumors . . ." said Terry quietly.

"You've heard that the senator had a daughter—that is an illegitimate daughter born to another woman before his marriage?"

"Somethin' like that," said Terry. "The senator was— Well, he was always troubled about somethin' from his past that might come out and embarrass him."

"Quit playing games, Terry," said Kennelly. "This is what might get you out of jail. If you know anything about this, you had better tell it."

Terry Rolland rubbed her wrists as if the handcuffs had been too tight and had chafed her skin. "You know the Latin word *paterfamilias*?" she asked. "It means a father. But more than just a father. It means a man who is head of a household, and not only that but dominates the household. That's how Huey was. Huey dominated all his people, like he was their father. Some people he dominated tough. Like me. He treated me like a daughter, some ways. A lot of ways, in fact."

"Yeah. Oh, yeah," sneered Kennelly. "And he made you do sixty days on a prison farm."

"You want to know why? I made a big declaration of independence. I told him to go to hell. To his face, I told him— I . . . I was too big a girl to spank, too big to send to bed without my supper. Yes, he sent me to the parish farm. But you know something? It was because he cared about me. The man cared for me. I always *knew* he did. I had to believe he did. He gave me an awful hard time, some ways. But when he died, I felt like my whole world had come to an end."

"Was this girl his daughter?" Kennelly demanded, tapping the birth certificate with one finger.

Terry stared again at the document. Then she nodded. "He was awful drunk one night, and he told me. It was— It was with her like it was with me, only more. He loved her. But he wanted her to— He wanted her to leave this country and live in Europe. He said he'd bring her back after he became President of the United States and make her a *princess*."

"He couldn't run for president if the word got out that he had an illegitimate child," said Szczygiel.

Terry nodded. "Don't reckon he could."

"This daughter didn't dare go back to Louisiana, I'd guess," said Kennelly.

Terry sighed. "He was elected governor in 1928, you remember. That's when he got the idea she should live in Europe. His idea was that he could hide her over there and nobody here would ever know about her. He sent her to a high-falutin' boardin' school up in New England to get her ready to live in England or somewheres—because he did love her and wanted things to be right for her. When he came to Washington in 1931, she was just nineteen. He sent her to Bryn Mawr." Terry shook her head. "It was a big mistake. The more education she got, the more she learned about her father. They had some kind of argument. He wanted her to go back home. She wouldn't. He cut off her money. And that was another big mistake."

"If she gone back to Louisiana, she'd have wound up on a prison farm like you did," said Kennelly.

Terry shook her head. "Maybe in an insane asylum."

"Oh, dear!" said Mrs. Roosevelt.

"He was with her like he was with me. As long as she did what he told her, everythin' was okay. When she didn't . . ." She shook her head and sighed. "I don't know what kind of fight they had, what was said. I never saw her. All I know is what he told me . . . plus what Paul Duroc said."

"Do you mean to say," asked the First Lady, "that he would have put her away in a *mental institution*?"

"Are you naive enough to think psychiatry is a science?" Terry asked. "He could have hired six psychiatrists to testify she was hopelessly insane—the same as he could have hired six to testify she was perfectly normal."

Kennelly shook his head. "Never mind that— What did Duroc know about her?"

"I don't know. He mentioned her. He knew she existed."

"You understand she is dead," said Mrs. Roosevelt.

Terry looked at Kennelly. "Was she the picture you shown me?"

Kennelly nodded.

Terry sighed. "Murdered. I'm glad Huey didn't live to see his daughter murdered."

"She was a hooker," said Kennelly. "Part of the time, anyway. Did he know that?"

"I don't believe it," said Terry firmly.

"She was living with Paul Duroc," said Kennelly.

"In the house on Columbia Road? That was his love nest."

"Did you ever go there?"

"Not voluntarily," said Terry.

"But you did go?"

"Whatta you want me to do, give you a motive for why I could've killed him?"

"We have ample evidence, Terry," said Mrs. Roosevelt, "to prove that Antonia Long lived with Paul Duroc in the house on Columbia Road. There is also, unhappily, incontrovertible evidence that she worked as a prostitute, in a house of ill repute. Now, if you can add any word to explain those facts, please do so."

Terry Rolland shook her head. "I can't believe it. Huey loved her. He gave her money. Why would she—? No. There's somethin' wrong here."

"Let's get some things straight," said Kennelly. "You say you never met Antonia Long, never met her?"

"No."

"Did you know the name: Antonia?"

Terry shook her head. "I never heard her called that. I heard her called Toni. That's the only name I ever heard for her: Toni Long. And I only heard that name spoken two or three times."

Kennelly looked to Mrs. Roosevelt and shrugged. "I guess we might as well take Terry back, then."

Mrs. Roosevelt shook her head. "I'm afraid you must."

"Put your jacket on, Terry," said Kennelly. "It's cold out."

The young woman picked up the tattered denim jacket, stared at it distastefully, and pulled it on over her jail dress. She offered her hands glumly, and Kennelly locked the handcuffs on her wrists again.

"Another reason for coming," said Kennelly. "I did get the report from the ballistics boys. The twenty-five-caliber pistol that killed the pawnbroker is the same one that killed Antonia Long. That's progress, huh?"

Focused as her attention was on the solution of the mystery that now encompassed three murders, Mrs. Roosevelt was still First Lady, and her position would have entailed many responsibilities even had she not chosen to have as active a personal agenda as she did.

She could not sit in her study and contemplate the chart she had made. She had to dress and leave the White House at six-thirty to attend a dinner at the Hay-Adams Hotel.

Since the first appearance of her column a few months ago, she had enjoyed gratifying acceptance in the exclusive fraternity of newspaper columnists. A few sniffed that she could not earn money writing columns if she were not First Lady, but most of the established columnists welcomed her, and some even sent her tips on how to improve her writing.

Tonight a group of columnists were meeting for dinner at the Hay-Adams, and Mrs. Roosevelt was genuinely pleased to have been invited.

All of them treated her politely, even those who most scorned her husband, even a few who had taken shots at her personally.

Arthur Brisbane, the pompous, turgid, moralizing sooth-sayer for William Randolph Hearst, had accused the New Deal of leading the country down the road to communism, but he was patrician enough to treat the First Lady with genteel civility.

"I enjoyed your column about the dogs on the *Queen Mary*, Mr. Brisbane," she told him.

A news story had appeared saying that on the luxurious new ship there would be special staterooms for passengers' dogs, and some had criticized this, calling it decadent coddling of the rich.

"With all this coddling, the dogs are still dogs," Brisbane had written, "just as the do-gooder who thinks he can change the world overnight is still a goose."

Mrs. Roosevelt chose to overlook the fact that the "goose" to which Brisbane had referred had the initials FDR.

Brisbane understood, and his cheeks were a bit pinker as he bowed slightly and said he was happy she had enjoyed the column.

Heywood Broun was at the opposite side of the political spectrum. Though possessed of a sharp but gentle wit, he was a big, graceless elephant of a man, of whom Dorothy Parker had written that he reminded her of "an unmade bed." He had once written that the dirty work of the New Deal was done at night, when New Dealers sneaked out with fists full of white chalk and wrote "Capitalism Must be Destroyed" on Washington sidewalks.

That evening Mrs. Roosevelt was introduced to a new columnist, Drew Pearson, who wrote "The Washington Merry-Go-Round"—a daily mishmash of gossip and conjecture with an occasional gem of real reporting. Westbrook Pegler was there. He was an old friend but had begun to become disenchanted with the Roosevelt administration.

The First Lady was pleased to hear that Louella Parsons,

though invited, had not appeared. Her Hollywood swill was nauseating.

Mrs. Roosevelt was not asked to speak. In this society she was a very junior member. She sat beside a young journalist at dinner, was fascinated by him, and would always remember him. His name was Ernie Pyle.

XII

"What the evidence points to is all but totally inconceivable," Mrs. Roosevelt said to the President in his bedroom on Saturday morning. "Yet, it is evidence."

The President sat propped up in bed, his back resting against a stack of pillows. As always at that time of day, he was surrounded by newspapers. His breakfast tray was on his lap. Fala scampered around the bed, happy and yapping. The President tossed him another crumb of toast, which the Scottie leaped to catch.

"Why couldn't somebody have told me this when Huey was alive?" the President asked.

"Franklin, it is a personal tragedy, with more than political significance," she protested.

"Oh, of course, of course. I'm sitting here reading the accounts of the League of Nations' denunciation of Hitler's remilitarization of the Rhineland. Which Hitler will ignore. I have to think about the way the Senate rejected the League. I have to wonder how it would have been if the

United States had joined. I'm sorry, but I can't give very much thought to the problems generated by the late Huey Long—that is, I can't now that he's dead. Do you mean to say his daughter was a prostitute?"

Mrs. Roosevelt sighed. "So it would appear. I can't imagine— Franklin, I simply can't imagine why. I've heard some perfectly terrible things."

"I'll give you a suggestion, Babs," said the President. "Question him gently."

"You mean . . . Louis?"

The President nodded. "There wasn't much in this world of politics that Louie Howe didn't know. Jim Farley is good, but Louie . . . Louie knew everything. He made it his business to know everything, and what Louis McHenry Howe made it his business to do, *he did*."

"I am reluctant to trouble him."

"*Trouble him!* Nothing will kill Louie quicker than getting to feel he's useless. You'll make the old boy happy, going to see him, asking him for the straight stuff on a character like Huey Long. I bet Louie carries in a file in that gray head of his enough information to have crucified Huey Long, if he'd lived."

"Crucified?"

"No. That was how Our Savior died. No. If Huey had lived to run for President in 1936, Louie Howe would have shoved him headfirst down the hole under an outhouse. Where he would have been right at home."

"Oh, Franklin!"

The President picked up a newspaper. "Louie. Talk to Louie. Uh . . ." He lowered the newspaper and closed his eyes. "While you can," he said softly.

* * *

"You're looking so much better this morning," she said to Louis McHenry Howe. "I'm so pleased."

Howe was weak. He sighed. "They won't let me smoke. What difference could it make now?"

"A great deal of difference, Louis," she said gently. "We want you back at the White House, back in the campaign."

Howe shook his head. "I'm on my last legs, Eleanor," he said in his small, ravaged voice. "I won't *be* back."

"Let's pray it isn't so," said Mrs. Roosevelt, struggling not entirely successfully to control her voice.

Howe reached up and touched a tear on her cheek. "All things come to an end," he said. "Think of it. If they didn't, we'd have to live with them forever. The alternative to death is eternal life—eternal life in *this* world, that is. I've enjoyed this life, on the whole. But I've reached the point when there's no joy left in it."

"The joy of satisfaction in a life's work well done," the First Lady suggested.

"Oh, yes. And it *is* done. So . . . I sense— I have a sense that you have a little work yet for me."

"Louis . . . Until the last hour, Franklin and I will look to you as our friend, our very best friend, with something still to contribute to *our* work."

Howe reached for her hand. He smiled. "Which makes it okay," he said. " 'Never retired. Helped as he could with his last breath.' An obit, Eleanor. I couldn't ask for a better one. So . . . I bet you didn't come to bring me a basket of fruit, God forbid. What can I do for you?"

"You know that Paul Duroc was murdered with poison on the second floor of the West Wing last week."

Howe nodded.

"Did you know that Senator Long had an illegitimate daughter?"

Howe smiled faintly. "I was holding that one for, say, September, maybe October. Sure. Antonia Caroline Long. The information is in my files, Eleanor. For God's sake, read my files! I can't tell you everything!"

"Did you know that young woman was murdered?"

"No!"

"Did you know she was a prostitute?"

Louis Howe coughed into his fist—deeply, painfully, and he needed a moment to recover. "Well, maybe," he said. "That depends on how you define the word. She did it, but she wasn't committed to it."

"Why?"

"There is a simple reason," said Howe, "and a not-so-simple reason. The simple reason is that Huey gave her money and then withheld money, depending on— Well . . . Depending on whim. Uh, she . . . We have to face a fact about Antonia, Eleanor. She blackmailed Huey. She knew she could destroy him politically. She was, incidentally, called Toni, not Antonia."

"How many people knew about her?" asked Mrs. Roosevelt.

"Just about nobody," said Howe. "If you went down to Louisiana and looked for her birth certificate, you wouldn't find it. Odd thing. The St. Martin Parish courthouse burned down in 1929, with all the records. The state record— Purged."

"She offered a copy of her birth certificate when she applied for a passport early this week."

Howe smiled and nodded. "Her mother was as smart as Huey. Smarter. She got copies of the little girl's birth certificate and sent them to safe places, before Huey became governor. There's a birth certificate for Antonia Caroline Long in my files. And where do you think I got it?"

"From—"

"Antonia Matilde Boudreau. She lives in Florida, on the income from a trust fund Huey set up for her. Well— Actually, certain Louisiana highway contractors endowed the fund. That makes no difference. She used the birth certificates to make sure Huey did his duty by her and by their daughter. And a year ago, when Huey began to make noises about running for President, she sent a copy to me. She sent a letter to her daughter, telling her I had a copy of the birth certificate. Antonia telephoned me. We talked about two minutes, on two occasions. When Huey died, there was no longer any reason for us to be in contact."

"Are you saying the mother and daughter didn't want the senator to become President?"

"Absolutely. He'd used his power as governor to destroy the record of his daughter's birth. The mother felt it was not safe for her to live in Louisiana anymore. The daughter felt the same way. They were afraid of how he'd use his power against them if he became President of the United States."

"Then, why in the world did Antonia Long practice prostitution in Washington?" asked Mrs. Roosevelt, shaking her head. "If there was a trust fund—"

"I didn't say Miss Boudreau lives in luxury," said Howe.

"But, Louis—"

"Simple reason, plus maybe a not-so-simple reason," said Howe. "It would have been one thing for Huey to have to explain an illegitimate daughter. He might have explained that away reasonably well. He had, after all, sent her to a boarding school, to college, and so on. But how would he explain an illegitimate daughter who was a hooker?"

"You mean she did it so as more effectively to put pressure on the senator to give her an allowance? It seems farfetched."

"I don't know that," Howe interrupted. "Speculation. But informed speculation. Intelligent speculation, if you don't mind my saying so."

"Would Paul Duroc have known all about this?"

Howe nodded. "If anyone in Washington besides me knew about it, Paul Duroc would have been the one."

"She lived with him in his house on Columbia Road," said Mrs. Roosevelt. "She had access to his safe-deposit box that had more than fifty thousand dollars in it."

"They were working together, then," said Howe. "Maybe Huey was more a victim than we ever guessed."

Back in her study, Mrs. Roosevelt looked through the small file she kept on the Duroc-Long murders and found what she was looking for: the telegram dated September 8, 1935, that had been found in Paul Duroc's bedroom—

HUEY SHOT THIS EVENING IN CAPITOL ROTUNDA STOP WOUND SERIOUS
BUT PROBABLY NOT FATAL STOP CONDUCT YOURSELF AS IF IT IS FATAL
STOP GET THIS WORD TO TL IMMEDIATELY STOP

O.K.

It made more sense now. O.K. was O. K. Allen, Huey Long's handpicked successor as governor. TL could be Toni Long. Duroc should get word to Toni that her father had been shot.

*   *   *

"Mr. Szczygiel," said Mrs. Roosevelt, "I believe you said a person's fingerprint files are not checked before that person is given employment in the White House."

"That's right. The Secret Service recommends it, but since so many of those people come on the recommendation of political friends of the man in the Oval Office it's not done. Never has been."

"And by the same token, we don't take their fingerprints after they are employed?"

Szczygiel shook his head. "I wish we did."

"What is more," she said, "relatively few of the employees on the White House clerical staff are civil service employees."

Szczygiel nodded. "The theory is the same throughout the government. People who work closely with high officials, including members of Congress, are exempted from the civil service laws. The theory is that high officials should be able to hire people in whom they have personal confidence."

"Well, everything related to Paul Duroc is an appropriate subject for our curiosity," said the First Lady. "I took the liberty of calling for Miss Sandra Wilson's personnel file. It appears she is exactly what you said: a secretary hired because she was the girl Paul Duroc wanted. She did not come from the civil service pool, and we know very little about her."

"If you don't mind my sounding priggish, I'd say we know one thing about her," said Szczygiel.

"And that is?"

"She bleaches her hair and makes herself up to look like Jean Harlow," said Szczygiel. "Well, that's all right for Jean Harlow, but I'm just old-fashioned enough to believe the secretaries around the White House should dress and act like secretaries and not like sexy movie stars."

"That's probably what Paul Duroc liked about her," laughed Mrs. Roosevelt. "What I'd like to know is who she is and where she came from. And that's not in her file."

Szczygiel raised his eyebrows. "A theory of the case?"

"No," said the First Lady. "I thought, though, that it is a cardinal principal of criminal investigation that the investigator should accumulate all possible facts. Should we neglect any facts just because we don't immediately see their relevance?"

"You will have to ask Kennelly," said Szczygiel. "He's the expert on criminal investigation."

A new organization called Government Girls had invited the First Lady to be their guest for a box lunch at the YWCA. Of course she attended. Lorena Hickock, who worked for the government, went with her. There were to be no speakers. The subject of the meeting was the cost of living and wages.

Mrs. Roosevelt and Lorena Hickock insisted on paying for their own box lunches, even if they were guests: five cents for a ham-and-cheese sandwich and an apple, with coffee available from an urn.

The government girls had arranged a display of ads and photographs to show what prices they had to pay. One of them asked the First Lady to pay particular attention to an enlarged photograph of the window of an A & P store.

Coffee at that store—the A & P house brand, ground to order—was two pounds for thirty-five cents. A pound of store cheese, advertised as made from whole milk, sold at twenty-three cents a pound. A dozen bars of Palmolive soap cost forty-nine cents. A bottle of ketchup cost a dime. Eggs were twenty-nine cents a dozen. A can of apple sauce cost seven cents. A box of macaroni cost a nickel. For seventeen cents you could buy three pounds of tomatoes. Del Monte peas sold at two cans for twenty-seven cents. Fancy creamery butter was thirty-seven cents a pound. A dozen rolls of toilet tissue cost twenty-nine cents.

"I make twelve dollars a week," the young woman told Mrs. Roosevelt. "My half of the rent for the rooms me and my roommate live in is three dollars and twenty-five cents a week. When I leave the grocery store, there's hardly anything left of a five-dollar bill. Carfare to work and back is sixty cents a week. I can hardly buy a dress for less than six or eight dollars, or a pair of shoes for less than four. It costs twenty cents to go to a movie." She shook her head. "You see what I mean?"

"I do indeed," said Mrs. Roosevelt. "Wages for government employees should be coupled to the cost of living, so that when prices increase wages automatically increase too. But it is the Congress which must so decide."

She did not say to the young woman something else that was on her mind: that in this inflationary economy where people had such difficulty in making ends meet the Dow-Jones Industrial Average was above 100!

Stan Szczygiel went home in the middle of that Saturday afternoon. He guessed he might be called on to work that night, and he decided he was entitled to a couple hours' rest.

Wilma was there. She had moved in with him Thursday, and to his surprise had proved to be a conscientious housekeeper. Modestly dressed in sweater and skirt, she looked like anything but a girl he had taken from a bawdy house only two nights before.

"Hey, Wilma," he said, "we now know who Claudia Jordan really was."

"I knew she wasn't Claudia Jordan."

"She was Huey Long's illegitimate daughter."

Wilma whistled. "Jeez! The Kingfish's daughter! Working as a whore! What's the world coming to?"

"You didn't know?"

"I swear. But maybe . . . maybe Bess knew. There was something about those two that used to make me think they were more than just madam and hooker."

"Like what?"

"Oh, like soulful conversations. It was like they had some kind of business together. And sometimes they came in together, like they had been someplace together."

"You told us Paul Duroc carried a gun. Do you have any idea why?"

"I can only tell you one thing. The guy was paranoid. Isn't that the word for a guy who always thinks somebody's out to get him? He was always peeking out the windows—I mean, from behind the closed shades. I got so I was scared of him."

Ed Kennelly and Lee Slusser waited in a parked car on East Executive Avenue. The radio call came at 5:32.

"Car twelve, car twelve. Your subject has left her office."

Secret Service Agent Deconcini had telephoned headquarters to report that Sandra Wilson was leaving the White House. The radio dispatcher had passed the information on to the two detectives in the car.

Slusser spotted her in Lafayette Park. He followed her.

The young woman walked fast, with long strides, her heels clicking on the pavement of the walk. At the corner of Connecticut and H she stopped and bought a hot dog from a vendor. She ate it as she walked on, stopping before she reached Eye to toss the paper into a can.

On Eye Street she walked half a block, then turned into the Farragut Bar. Slusser went to a police call box and reported to headquarters. Headquarters radioed his report to Kennelly. The report wasn't necessary, actually. Kennelly had been following in the car and pulled up to the call box within two minutes.

"She might recognize me," said Kennelly. "You go in and see what's up."

Slusser went in and returned in a minute or so.

"It's dark in there. She's sitting in the rear. You can come in if you want."

Kennelly followed Slusser back inside the Farragut Bar. The two detectives took places at the bar near the front and ordered beer.

The Farragut Bar was well known to Kennelly. It was a short walk, not just from the White House but from major government departments, and it was a favorite watering hole for weary government workers who wanted to unwind with a drink or two before going home. It was usually crowded in early evening and again late in the evening when couples who had gone to movies came in for a drink after the show. The decor was supposed to be nautical. The waitresses wore yachting caps, blue jackets, and short white skirts. Three bartenders were busy filling orders.

Sandra Wilson was not alone. She sat at a table with another young woman and two young men. That they were two couples and who was matched with whom was entirely apparent.

"H'lo, Kennelly," said the chief bartender, a heavy man with a long white apron tied around his waist. He brought their beers, though they had given their order to another bartender. "Relaxin' or workin'?"

"A little bit of each," said Kennelly.

"Anything I can do for ya?"

"Yeah. Jean Harlow back there. Know her?"

The bartender glanced at Sandra Wilson. "I don't know her. She's not the kind of girl you wouldn't notice, though, is she? I mean, look at that bleach job! And that figure! Anyway, she comes in once in a while. Always with the guy. Same guy. She's not a hooker."

"How long has she been coming in?"

"Oh, I don't know, exactly. I'd guess four, five months. That's just a guess."

"You know who the guy is?"

"Nope. I've never seen him without her. They're a pair, I guess. I betcha they're goin' to a picture show. Seven o'clock show. They'll have a couple drinks each and leave. That's what they do. They come in for a couple drinks about six, then leave. I betcha they go to the movies. Twice a week."

"They don't drink much, then?"

The bartender shook his head. "No. They're nice kids, far as I can make out. Never had a problem with 'em. They're not loud. No kind of fuss."

"What's she drink, you know?" Kennelly asked.

"I don't know. I can ask."

"Without her knowing you asked," said Kennelly.

The bartender walked down the bar, spoke to a waitress,

and returned. "Bourbon," he said. "Not just bar whiskey, either. She likes Old Granddad. Always orders it."

Kennelly grinned. "Robert, my friend, I appreciate your help."

He shoved a quarter across the bar to pay for the two beers, but the bartender smiled, shook his head, and shoved it back.

"I ought to be mad at you, Stan," said Bess. "For taking Wilma away from me, I mean. You left me short. I only have one girl working tonight."

"I can't say I'm sorry. Frankly, I don't think Wilma belonged in this kind of life," said Szczygiel solemnly. "She's a nice girl. The Depression—"

"Sure," Bess interrupted. "The Depression. Every whore has a sob story. It's one of the tricks of the trade. Every John a girl sees asks her what a nice girl like her is doing in a business like this, and ninety percent of them today will talk about the Depression."

"Okay. If you say so."

"Look, I'm not mad at you for taking Wilma. I hope she goes to Florida with you. I hope she never comes back. Hey, Stan . . . I even hope her story is true, that she was forced into this by the Depression. Any time a girl can escape from this life, I'm for her."

Bess drew a deep breath. She was asthmatic, and sucking a breath deep into her soft bulk was a labor for her. "Well, I guess you didn't come by to be sociable. What can I do for you?"

"We know who Claudia Jordan was," said Szczygiel.

Bess nodded. "Yeah? Good. Who was she?"

"I suspect you know."

"I didn't have anything to do with her getting killed," said Bess quickly.

"I don't suppose you did. But you knew who she was, didn't you?"

Bess sighed. "Toni came here about a year ago, wanted to work. Like I told you Thursday night, she was not the type I usually see. I mean, she was high-toned. I didn't figure she'd stay, but she did. She worked like any other girl. For a while. I got to know her. You know, you sit around waiting a lot in this business; and I spent a lot of time with her. One thing I asked her pretty soon was, why'd she come to me? A girl like her could've worked in a posh place. She said she was afraid somebody she knew would see her. I still didn't know who she was then. It was odd. She didn't seem to have any friends. Not in Washington, anyway."

"How and when did you find out who she was?"

"I gotta ask a question, Stan," Bess wheezed. "Can I trust you to keep some things quiet? If Kennelly found out about some of this, I could—"

"You tell me," said Szczygiel. "I'll let Kennelly find out for himself."

"Toni had a problem," Bess said solemnly. "She took dope. She smoked reefers and she used something that she shot into herself with a needle. That was why she needed money so bad as to bring her to me. Her father knew about it, I think. Sometimes he gave her enough money to buy the stuff, and sometimes he didn't. She was hiding here. But she had to have money and go out and buy her stuff. That's why she worked."

"How could this information get you in trouble?" asked Szczygiel.

"Well . . . She used the stuff here. I was supposed to turn her in, wasn't I?"

Ed Kennelly sat down in Stan Szczygiel's kitchen. Wilma poured drinks for the three of them: gin for Stan, whiskey for herself and Kennelly.

"It explains a lot, if it's true," said Kennelly. "How about it, Wilma? Is it true?"

"I smelled the reefers," said Wilma. "I've never touched it, but I know the smell of the smoke from Mary Jane. A lot of whores use it. And worse. I never saw Claudia . . . Toni use anything else. She'd have done that in private."

Szczygiel looked at his watch. "I think we'd better call Mrs. Roosevelt," he said. "It's late, but I think you'd better tell her what you saw at the Farragut Bar, and I'd better tell her what Bess said. It's late, but she won't like it if we wait till morning. Anyway, with that mind of hers rolling all this stuff over and over, by tomorrow she may be able to tell us who killed who and why."

"Okay," said Kennelly. "And afterward, would you like to go with me and see some down-and-dirty police work?"

"In one way," said Kennelly as he pulled the car to the curb on F Street, "this is a shot in the dark. In another way it's damned promising. We have to test our luck."

A light snow had begun to fall. Lights glistened on it. Like snow always mysteriously does, this snow muffled sound. The after-midnight street was unnaturally quiet.

Both men wore overcoats and hats. Szczygiel twitched his left shoulder. He was not used to carrying a revolver in a shoulder holster and was uncomfortable with it. Kennelly had issued it to him at police headquarters.

"We walk," said Kennelly.

They left the car and walked east on F Street, past the Pennsylvania Hotel, toward Union Station. At this time of night parties of revelers were returning to their hotels—the Wallick and Commodore were close by the Pennsylvania. Others were on the streets: drunks, derelicts, hookers, even panhandlers still at work.

"Y' want an honest answer to an honest question, y' ask somebody who's got a motive to give it to you—" said Kennelly as he approached a tall, light-skinned colored woman who had the posture and gestures of a hooker. "Hey, kid. What's the deal?"

"Fav," she said. Five. "The very best."

"Whatta ya do for two dollars?"

"I ain't," she said. "I ain't no two-dollah who'."

"I bet you're not," said Kennelly. He showed her his badge.

"Hey! You got it wrong, policeman. You ast me what I do for two dollah, and I say I ain't—"

"Yeah, but you are for five. Never mind. I don't care about that. You get no hassle from me. I want an honest answer to an honest question."

She lifted her chin high. "I bet it ain't no easy question," she muttered.

"I bet it ain't either," said Kennelly. "But I bet you got the answer."

"Try me."

"Suppose I wanted to smoke some Mary Jane. Where'd I get it, huh?"

"Sheet, Mistah Policeman. I don't do that."

"Didn't say you did. But somebody on this street, or right

around here, sells it. All I wanta know is who. You work this
street, you know. All secret. Between you and me."

"Nevah let it be said I didn't help out the law when I
could."

"So help now."

"Don' know," she said emphatically. "Nevah wanted any.
'Fraid of it. But I know a gal who uses some. Name of Sis.
That's all the name I got for her: Sis. I c'n tell you where to
find her. Union Station. She not allow inside. Find her outside. May not be there this time of night."

"What's she look like?"

The prostitute grinned. "Sheet! Don' all of us look alike
to you, white man?"

"*You* don't," said Kennelly.

"Okay. Darker'n me. Shorter. Fatter. I seen her while ago.
She got on a green knit hat, what you call a beret. You don'
mention me, right?"

They walked to the station. The prostitute called Sis was
standing in the shadows just beyond the taxi stand. Kennelly walked up to her and showed his badge. The conversation was brief. In the end she named and described the man
who sold her marijuana.

The Wallick Hotel was in an old tradition. Above the
lobby was a mezzanine floor, meaning that the ceiling of the
central lobby was twenty-five feet above the marble floor.
Marble columns supported the mezzanine. Great potted
palms flourished, as did smaller shrubs in brass tubs all
around the lobby. Cigar-smoking men in overcoats and hats
still sat in big, worn, leather-covered chairs, each one with
a tall brass spittoon beside it. Though the Negro women
from the street were not allowed inside the hotel, three
young white women sitting on a leather-covered bench by

the bell captain's station were obviously prostitutes waiting for an approach or call. The news and cigar stand was still open.

Kennelly strode to the captain's station. "H'lo, Willy."

"Lieutenant," said the bell captain, conspicuously unhappy to see the police detective.

"Bobby," said Kennelly.

The bell captain shrugged and shook his head.

"Wil-ly . . ."

"You didn't get it from me. Camel overcoat. Black hat."

"Dealer in . . . odd substances, Willy?"

"I wouldn't know. But I wouldn't be surprised."

"Thanks, Willy. Friends as always."

"Kennelly . . ."

"Yeah."

"One friend to another. He's carryin' heat."

The man in the handsome camel overcoat and black homburg, wearing also a paisley silk scarf, maroon and olive-green, was six feet one and well put together. Kennelly guessed he was thirty years old.

"Y' know how to work this, Stan?"

Szczygiel shook his head.

Kennelly told him how to work it, and they walked across the lobby to the man called Bobby. Just as the detective lieutenant came within what the man might have considered the area of his territorial imperative, Kennelly showed him the muzzle of a snub-nose .38 revolver. It was in his right hand. His badge was thrust forward in his left.

"Don't move, Bobby. Hands behind your back."

The man hesitated for an instant, then put his hands back. Szczygiel seized first one hand and then the other and snapped handcuffs on him.

"What the hell is this?"

Kennelly reached inside the man's overcoat and jacket and found a pistol, an Iver-Johnson revolver. "Concealed weapon. We can start with that. Now what else we got?"

He went into the man's overcoat pockets.

"My God," said Kennelly. "What's in all these little packages, Bobby?"

Half an hour later, Bobby—his last name was Basrak—sat stark naked on a chair in an interrogation room at D.C. police headquarters. His hands were cuffed to the arms of the chair.

His face was pocked. His naked body was thin and pallid.

"On the evidence we found on you, Bobby, plus the evidence we can pick up easy, you're lookin' at, what, twenty years to life? You want any less than that? Talk!"

"I get the stuff here and there, from guys. They don't give me their names, and I don't give them mine."

"That's not what I want to know, Bobby," said Kennelly. "I know you might not live long in the place if you give me those names. I got somethin' else in mind. Somethin' else entirely."

Szczygiel nudged Kennelly. "Don't, for God's sake, let Mrs. R. find out your interrogation methods."

"I only use it on crumb bums," said Kennelly.

XIII

The First Lady received telephone calls from Stan Szczygiel and Ed Kennelly early on Sunday morning. They reported all they had learned the night before.

"I believe," she said, "we have all the information we need to resolve the question of who murdered Paul Duroc and Antonia Long. I am thinking of calling one of those perhaps-overdramatic meetings and letting a great many people confront each other. That has sometimes proved an effective way of solving mysteries, has it not?"

She said this during her conversation with Kennelly, and he agreed it was often a very effective way of getting to the bottom of a mystery.

"On the other hand," she said later to Szczygiel, "I do not propose to call such a meeting on Sunday. I suggest you take the day off, Mr. Szczygiel. You've been keeping late hours."

Leaving her bedroom, Mrs. Roosevelt stopped to say good-morning to the President. She found he was up and dressed and was not in his bedroom but in the adjacent oval study, grim-faced and facing an equally grim Harold Ickes, Secretary of the Interior.

"Am I intruding on something?" she asked.

"Intrude if you wish," said the President. "We're just going over some of the news stories from the flood."

Ickes handed her a thick file of newspaper clippings.

A headline from Friday's *New York Times* read—

FLOOD TOLL TO 29,
NEW ENGLAND LOSS
PUT AT $50,000,000

Record-breaking floods on the Connecticut and Merrimac rivers, among others, were inundating the big New England mill towns, closing factories and throwing tens of thousands out of work. Boats of the New England fishing fleet were ranging many miles inland on the flood waters, rescuing stranded families, some of them from rooftops. Bridges were down, highways and railroads were washed out, and miles of utility wires were on the ground and under water.

But it was not just New England that was suffering. The *Pittsburgh Sun-Telegraph* reported that a huge boiler at a Jones & Laughlin steel mill had exploded when an emergency dike ruptured and submerged the furnace and boiler under muddy water. Released pressure shot steam, flame, and debris thousands of feet. Pittsburgh's downtown Golden Triangle was under eight feet of floodwater.

In Portsmouth, Ohio, the floodwaters reached the top of

a forty-foot-high floodwall. The city engineers opened floodgates and let the water enter the city's underground storm-sewer system, to prevent the collapse of the wall. The sudden intense pressure hurled manhole covers fifty feet in the air.

"I have ordered sandbag dikes put up around the Lincoln Memorial," the President said. "It is possible the Potomac will reach that high."

The First Lady shook her head. "Thousands of people out of work," she said. "Thousands of homes destroyed. The government must help, Franklin."

"That's what Harold and I are talking about," said the President.

"Republicans in the Congress insist that coping with natural disasters is none of the government's business," said Secretary Ickes. "Republicans . . . Many Democrats."

"Surely helping people who are suffering is the government's business," said Mrs. Roosevelt. "Isn't that in fact what nearly all of our new programs are for?"

"Hear, hear," said the President wearily.

"The problem," said Ickes, "is getting an appropriation."

When Mrs. Roosevelt arrived at church she was greeted by the minister. She suggested to him that he should incorporate in his service a special prayer for the millions of people in the eastern half of the United States who were suffering from floods. He did.

Secret Service agents and detectives from District police spent several hours on Monday notifying people of the meeting Mrs. Roosevelt had arranged, to be held in the Cabinet Room at six o'clock.

Some came reluctantly. Some came in handcuffs. But none failed to appear. They were—

- Thérèse Rolland. She was brought to the White House in handcuffs, but Mrs. Roosevelt insisted that the handcuffs must be removed before she was brought into the Cabinet Room. She wore a black knit dress and a little pink lipstick.
- John Evans, Terry's lawyer, who sat beside her at the cabinet table. Wearing a double-breasted dark-blue suit, he appeared full of the bustling self-importance his detractors disliked in him.
- Daniel Selmer, the former aide to Huey Long. His beady brown eyes were unusually intense and shifted from one person to another, apparently searching.
- Samuel Paxton, the lobbyist for the Mississippi River-boatmen's Association. His gold-frame pince-nez in place, he glowered and twisted the ends of his great white mustache between the thumb and index finger of his right hand.
- Ernest McSweeney, the lobbyist for the sugar industry, looking calm and suave as always, white-haired, flushed of face, and wearing his red carnation.
- Bobby Basrak, the narcotics dealer arrested last night, in handcuffs and wearing jail dungarees.
- Sandra Wilson. She was conspicuously nervous. Her hair remained stripped of color, but she had perhaps wiped off most of her makeup for this meeting. She looked less Jean-Harlowish than she usually did. Instead, she looked timid and afraid.
- Stan Szczygiel.
- Ed Kennelly.
- Mrs. Roosevelt.

They sat around the table this way:

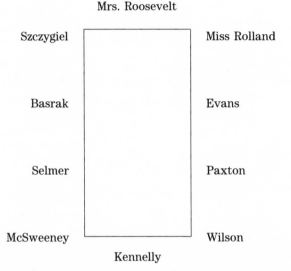

Mrs. Roosevelt

Szczygiel		Miss Rolland
Basrak		Evans
Selmer		Paxton
McSweeney		Wilson

Kennelly

A court-reporter stenographer sat at a small table to Mrs. Roosevelt's left, her fingers poised over her Stenograph machine. Dominic Deconcini sat on a chair against the wall and behind Sandra Wilson. Another agent sat behind Szczygiel.

"Ladies and gentlemen," said Mrs. Roosevelt, "I am painfully aware that summoning you to this meeting has been an imposition. I know you will understand that what we are trying to do is identify the murderer or murderers of two victims—and that may excuse us for so discommoding you. I hope it does. If we walk out of here an hour or so from now having failed to solve a mystery, I shall be most apologetic to you."

Samuel Paxton allowed his pince-nez to drop to the end of its ribbon. "For myself, Mrs. Roosevelt," he said, "I will not deny that it has been a considerable inconvenience to attend this meeting, whatever it is for. However—excuse me for beginning a sentence with 'however'—I for one am pleased to be here. If I can in any way assist you in solving the tragedy surrounding the deaths of these two young people, I shall be honored to have contributed my mite."

"Why, thank you, Mr. Paxton. I am afraid, however, that there are some people in this room who are appalled to be confronting each other. They had hoped never to see each other again."

Bobby Basrak glowered. He had no skill for concealing his thoughts or feelings.

"Where to begin?" asked Mrs. Roosevelt. "Well . . . I suppose it might be well to begin by identifying the unfortunate young woman who was murdered on F Street the night of last Wednesday and Thursday. We have a photograph of her face. Unfortunately, it is a morgue photograph, taken after she was dead. I will, even so, ask Lieutenant Kennelly to start it around the table. To your right, please, Lieutenant. First to Miss Wilson, then on up the table."

Sandra Wilson stared at the picture, then shook her head.

Samuel Paxton looked, shook his head and handed it to John Evans. He handed it to Terry, who also shook her head. She had seen it at the jail and had said then she didn't know the dead woman.

Mrs. Roosevelt passed it to Szczygiel, who passed it to Bobby Basrak.

For a moment the narcotics dealer stared at it. Then he said— "Yeah, sure. You sweated it outa me last night. She was a buyer."

"Meaning," said the First Lady, "that she bought dope from you?"

Basrak nodded. "I already gave the cops a statement. She bought Mary Jane from me for a while, then hard stuff."

"Hard stuff?"

"Stuff you shoot. Morphine. The strongest kind's called by a lot of bad names. I guess the polite name is heroin."

"Bobby's going away for a while," said Kennelly. "He's got it figured out that it's in his best interest to tell us everything he knows."

Mrs. Roosevelt nodded at Kennelly, and Kennelly took up the interrogation.

"Look around the table, Bobby," he said. "See anybody you ever saw before?"

Basrak, in his dungarees and handcuffs, was no longer the sleek, confident dealer he had been last night. He knew what he was facing. Under the law, a man could go to jail for years for selling heroin. On top of that he had been caught carrying a concealed weapon. He glanced nervously around the table.

"Yeah," he muttered. "Yeah, I know a guy. I know *this* guy."

He nodded at Daniel Selmer, who sat to his right.

Selmer spoke from between clenched teeth. "I never saw this man before in my life," he said.

"Selmer," said Kennelly, "in my years at the police department I've seen stupid murderers, but I don't think I ever saw one as stupid as you."

"This is outrageous!"

The Secret Service agent who had been sitting behind Szczygiel rose and stood behind Selmer.

"Almost everyone at this table knows who the murdered young woman was," said Mrs. Roosevelt. "If anyone does not, she was Antonia Caroline Long—usually known as

Toni—and she was the illegitimate daughter of Senator Huey Long. She was addicted to . . . to the substances Mr. Basrak sold her."

"Which was known to you, Selmer," said Kennelly. "Who told you she was an addict? Duroc? It took some little time and effort to locate her supplier. You had to ask around town. But you're a streetwise fellow and knew who to ask and what to ask. It took you a week, but eventually you located Bobby Basrak. He fingered Toni for you."

"Outrageous! Outrageous!" Selmer shrieked. "Why in the hell would I want to kill Toni Long?"

"To get the key to the safe-deposit box kept by Paul Duroc," said Mrs. Roosevelt.

"Safe-deposit box?"

"Where he kept the funds he had stolen from the Long campaign treasury," said the First Lady. "Not to mention other money he had received by falsifying the audits he did for the government. Paul Duroc had required very little time in Washington to make himself a wealthy man."

"All of this," said Selmer bitterly, "depends on the word of a confessed dope seller."

"The case might be tough to make if that were so," said Kennelly. "I said before, though, that you have to be the stupidest murderer I ever saw. Any kind of killer with any brains at all would get rid of the gun. But not you, buddy. I guess you thought you were so damned smart we would never catch up with you. So—"

Kennelly reached inside his jacket pocket and pulled out a tiny pistol: a .25-caliber Baby Browning automatic. He shoved it toward the middle of the table.

"It's yours, my boy," he said to Selmer. "We found it this afternoon in your house—searched incidentally, on the authority of a warrant we got this morning. Found in your house. Covered with your fingerprints. And the ballistics tests prove it was the pistol used to kill Toni Long. You're under arrest, in case you hadn't figured that out."

Selmer glanced around the table, from one face to another. "You'll never make it stick," he said. "That's my gun, for sure, but it was stolen from my house two weeks ago. I'll so testify. And . . . uh, uh, Sam Paxton will testify that I told him I was worried because my Baby Browning had been stolen. Isn't that right, Sam?"

Paxton nodded. "He did tell me that."

"I was worried it would be used to commit a crime," said Selmer.

"He told me that," said Paxton.

Kennelly bestowed a scornful glance on each of them. "Commit *crimes*," he said. "The same pistol was used to kill an elderly pawnbroker named Schmidt last Friday."

"So there you are," said Selmer. "My pistol was used to commit a street murder, then a robbery. Even if you can make a connection between me and Toni Long, you can't make one between me and some pawnbroker."

The meeting paused for a moment. The bald young Selmer fastened angry brown eyes on Kennelly and shook his head scornfully. The white-thatched Samuel Paxton hung his pince-nez on his nose and inspected the Baby Browning automatic with intent interest. John Evans whispered urgently in Terry Rolland's ear. Ernest McSweeney's attention seemed focused on the red carnation in his buttonhole. Sandra Wilson seemed unable to keep her lips together and glanced rapidly from one face to another.

"I am afraid the connection between you and the pawnbroker is a key," said Mrs. Roosevelt. "But I suggest, Lieutenant Kennelly, that we leave that for a few minutes. I believe you all know Mr. Szczygiel. He is an agent of the Secret Service. Crimes committed within the precincts of the White House are peculiarly within his jurisdiction. Mr. Szczygiel . . . why don't you proceed?"

Szczygiel stood. "A fact or two," he said. "Simple little facts that lead to bigger ones." He turned to Sandra Wilson. "You told us, Miss Wilson," he said, "that Paul Duroc once offered you a drink of bourbon but that you declined because you don't like bourbon. But . . . at the Farragut Bar, where you have a couple of drinks two or three times a week, you always order bourbon: Old Granddad, specifically."

"I didn't want to have a drink with Mr. Duroc," she said. "Having a drink with him would have led to . . . something else."

"Good enough," said Szczygiel. "Now, Miss Wilson, tell us at what hour you ordinarily leave the White House at the end of the day."

Sandra Wilson turned up the palms of her hands. "Six-thirty," she said. "Quarter to seven."

"In time to go to the Farragut Bar, have a drink or two, and still make the seven-o'clock movie?"

"Nights I go to the bar and to a movie with my boyfriend, I leave earlier."

"People who work in the West Wing say you are hardly ever seen in the wing after five-thirty."

"That's not right," she said. "I sometimes work much later than that."

Mrs. Roosevelt spoke. "On the evening of Wednesday, March fourth, you worked until seven o'clock, didn't you?"

"Yes. Mr. Duroc asked me to stay late enough to get some letters out."

Mrs. Roosevelt nodded. "Well . . . Lieutenant?"

Kennelly stood and went to the door. A moment later he led Florence Hennis into the Cabinet Room. "Miss Hennis," he said, "do you see anyone here that you know? I mean, do you see anyone you have seen before?"

The safe-deposit attendant from Farmers & Mechanics Bank glanced quickly around the table, then stared at each person. After a moment she nodded. "That one," she said, pointing at Sandra Wilson. "She wore a dark wig."

Sandra Wilson clapped her hands to her face and shrieked.

Samuel Paxton, who sat beside her, turned and grabbed her hands. "Easy, easy . . ." he said.

"The fact that you were gone from your new job in the West Wing for about an hour Friday morning is another suggestive circumstance," said Mrs. Roosevelt.

The young woman wept into her hands.

"Uh . . . Miss Hennis, if you would like to take a chair there by the wall and remain, we will be glad to have you. You may wish to know how this turns out."

Florence Hennis sat down behind Terry Rolland.

"Miss Wilson," said Mrs. Roosevelt gently. "You went to the Farmers and Mechanics Bank and signed out a safe-deposit box in the name of Elaine Curtis. Since there was no Elaine Curtis, maybe you were in fact the person who had used that name and were entitled to open the box. Many people keep boxes in false names, for a variety of reasons, not all of them illegal. So, tell us. What was in the box?"

Sandra Wilson had begun to cry. "Nothing," she sobbed. "It was empty!"

"All right, it was empty. That is because *we* had taken the money out of it. Does that answer a big question for you?"

Whether or not it answered a question for Sandra Wilson, it answered one for Dan Selmer, who suddenly flushed bright red.

Mrs. Roosevelt looked at Selmer. "Do you want to tell us the rest of it now, or shall we continue?"

Selmer grunted. "Let's hear what you know."

"We know who killed Paul Duroc," said the First Lady. "And how. And why."

Mrs. Roosevelt turned to Terry Rolland. "It wasn't you, Terry," she said.

Terry sighed. "That's what I've been telling you all along."

"You are no innocent. The time you've spent in jail was perhaps richly deserved. But you didn't murder Paul Duroc."

"Then who did?" asked Ernest McSweeney.

"Miss Sandra Wilson."

Ten minutes passed before they could continue. By then, Sandra Wilson, her hands locked behind her with the handcuffs Terry had worn, now sat quietly sobbing. Both Ed Kennelly and Dominic Deconcini had had to struggle to restrain her. Her shrill cries had reached all the way to the Oval Office, and Missy LeHand had come with the President's query as to what was going on in the Cabinet Room.

"Two people," said Mrs. Roosevelt, "had opportunity to introduce potassium cyanide into Paul Duroc's whiskey and water. Terry Rolland and you, Miss Wilson. You were in and out of his office all day, as your duties as his secretary required. You filled his carafes with coffee and ice water,

and you rinsed them out every morning before you refilled
them. You knew he drank his bourbon with water, because
you occasionally shared a drink with him. You told us you
disliked bourbon to cover the fact that you occasionally
drank from his office bottle. You answered his telephone,
got the information that Terry Rolland was coming over for
a drink, and you put the poison in the carafe. All the time
you needed was afforded by Duroc's leaving the office for
any reason. He went out for a moment—to speak to someone in another office, to go to the bathroom, whatever—and
you slipped into his office and poured the poison in his
water carafe."

"You're guessing," said Selmer morosely.

"To a degree," said Mrs. Roosevelt. "But let's follow the
story and see how the facts match. Terry Rolland could
have put the poison in Duroc's drink. But I have never
believed she did. In the first place, she would have had to
do it in Duroc's presence, since he did not leave the office
after she came in. What is more, it would have been stupid
for her to do it when she and he were alone in his office. The
murderers—and there are of course more than one—
wanted to create an appearance that Terry *had* to have
done it, that no one else could have. Lieutenant Kennelly
has characterized them as stupid. They have been stupid: in
creating a scenario that wholly depends on Terry Rolland's
being abysmally stupid, something we know she is not."

"Circumstantial evidence, I believe all this is called," said
Selmer. "And speculative. Highly speculative. Mr. Evans is
a lawyer. Isn't this called building an inference on an inference?"

Evans shrugged. "I represent Miss Rolland and am glad to

hear that the evidence lays the crime at someone else's door."

"What I should like to do now," said Mrs. Roosevelt, "is link the three murders, each to the other two. Maybe that, also, will be speculative, Mr. Selmer, but I think the linked murders build a tight case."

Selmer turned to Sandra Wilson. "Don't let them intimidate you," he said to her. "They've got no case at all."

"Paul Duroc," said the First Lady, "was a skilled auditor. He found faults in various accounts. When he did, he sometimes gave the subjects the choice of being exposed or of paying off. Captain Sykes and Congressman Devol, to cite one example, elected to pay off. At least their contractors did. We took their statements on that today. Duroc also knew about Antonia. He blackmailed Senator Long. The senator gave him access to campaign funds. Duroc pressured lobbyists and others to contribute generously to the Long campaign fund—and then stole much of the money for himself. This is how he filled a safe-deposit box with more than fifty thousand dollars in cash.

"When the senator was assassinated in Baton Rouge, Duroc hurried to grab whatever was left in the campaign fund," continued Mrs. Roosevelt. "There was not nearly as much as some of you thought—because he had already taken most of the money. You asked for your money back, Messieurs Paxton and McSweeney; and Duroc laughed at you. You asked for a share, Mr. Selmer, and he laughed at you."

Samuel Paxton turned down the corners of his mouth, and he shook his head ponderously. "It *is* speculation, dear lady," he said.

"That Sandra Wilson came to Farmers and Mechanics

Bank wearing a black wig *and carrying the key to the 'Elaine Curtis' box* removes the matter from the realm of speculation," said Mrs. Roosevelt. "Which one of them approached you, Miss Wilson?"

"Don't let her bluff you, Sandy," warned Daniel Selmer.

"As it stands, Miss Wilson," said Mrs. Roosevelt gently, "you alone are going to be charged with the murder of Paul Duroc. I point out to you that you are handcuffed. They are not."

Sandra Wilson swung her head back and forth. "I'm not going to take the fall," she sobbed. "I'm not going to be the only one."

"Sandy!"

"*He* came to me," she said, nodding toward Paxton.

Samuel Paxton shook his great head. "The young woman is hysterical," he declared.

"Not any longer, she isn't," said Mrs. Roosevelt. "I believe you can take the handcuffs off her, Lieutenant Kennelly."

Kennelly released the tearful young woman from the manacles. She put her hands over her face and wept quietly.

"I believe also you can advise Terry that she is no longer a prisoner."

Kennelly nodded. "You won't need to go back to jail," he said to Terry. "Not today anyway. When everything is straightened out, you may wind up inside again."

Sandra Wilson dropped her hands to her lap. Her face glistened with tears. She looked at Paxton. "He offered me five thousand dollars if I would slip a dose of poison into Mr. Duroc's water carafe. The way he described it, there wasn't the least possibility I could get caught." She pushed her chair down the table, to put a little more distance between herself and Samuel Paxton. "He's a smooth man, Mr. Paxton. I mean, he could make you believe the earth is square. Look at him . . . A damned Moses, Mr. Paxton. Who could think he could be wrong about anything? My first big mistake was—"

"You are making a terrible mistake now, Sandy!" Paxton roared. "Keep quiet! They can't prove these lies!"

"My first big mistake," she went on, "was in not demanding my money in advance. They didn't pay me. They said they couldn't until they found the deposit box and got it open."

"You came in early the next day," said Mrs. Roosevelt, "because the first thing you had to do was rinse out the water carafe. The police assumed that since the coffee carafe hadn't been emptied, the water carafe had not been disturbed either. They were wrong."

"When I came in Thursday morning, sure enough, the stale coffee was still in the one. I took the other to the ladies' room and washed it out. *Washed* it out, you can believe. And it seemed to be okay. It might have been, too, if they hadn't made me go to that bank and open that box."

"Anyone might have drunk water from that carafe," said Terry. "*I* might have."

Sandra Wilson shook her head with a small ironic smile. "You drink your whiskey neat," she said. "I saw you. More than once. It was Mr. Duroc who put water in his."

For a moment everyone was silent. Paxton, drawn up with indignation, stared at Sandra Wilson. Selmer glared at Paxton. Mrs. Roosevelt sat with her hands folded before her on the table. The stenographer took that moment to change the paper in her Stenotype.

"I've got some more of it figured out," said Kennelly. "One of you *bought* the cyanide from the pawnbroker,

Schmidt. Then he reported a can of it stolen, to cover himself. You didn't pay him either, 'cause you hadn't got the money out of the box, and he started to squawk. So you killed him."

"Sure, sure," sneered Selmer. "Dream on, Lieutenant."

"You'd never have seen your five thousand, Sandy," said Kennelly to Sandy. "They'd have killed you, too. There would have been no witnesses when it was all over."

"No, we wouldn't have," said Selmer. "Let me figure here. You have my pistol, with my fingerprints on it. Anybody else's prints, Lieutenant Kennelly?"

Kennelly shook his head. "Your fingerprints are on the cartridges in the clip, too. Nobody else's."

Selmer shook his head. "What the hell, Sam . . ." he muttered. "And Ernie," he added, nodding toward Ernest McSweeney. "Oh, yeah. All three of us."

"We figured that," said Kennelly.

McSweeney closed his eyes, clenched his hands together under his chin, and rested his chin on them. He emitted a long, noisy sigh. Paxton continued to glower.

"Okay . . ." said Selmer. "Well, little Miss Sandy Wilson isn't little Miss Sandy Wilson. She—"

"Selmer!" the young woman yelled.

"No, she isn't. Her name isn't Sandy Wilson, either. Her name is Angela Murphy. Yeah, Sam Paxton hired her. But not by stopping at her desk upstairs and politely asking her if she'd like to kill somebody. He hired her in New York and brought her to Washington. We had to pay her a thousand dollars in advance for her time and expenses. We knew how we wanted her to do it, and she agreed to it."

"How did you get her the job?"

"We knew Paul's secretary was leaving. She was getting

married. Ernie brought Sandy—Angela—in and introduced her to Paul. She was a good-enough stenographer and typist. She'd learned those skills in a girls' reformatory in New York. The other talent she needed to get her the job— Well, you know what I mean, and she had that in abundance."

Mrs. Roosevelt frowned. "How old are you, Miss . . . Murphy?"

Angela Murphy sneered. "Twenty-eight," she said.

"She's wanted for another murder," said Selmer.

"You son of a bitch!"

"The proposition was to bring her to Washington, set her up with a new identity, and pay her enough to make it possible for her to do whatever she wanted—maybe even leave the country. It wasn't five thousand, incidentally. It was ten. That's why we had to get the money from the box."

"I should like," said Mrs. Roosevelt, "to return to the subject of Antonia Long. I was under the impression that almost no one knew about her, yet all of you seem to have known. And Paul Duroc knew, obviously."

"She was his wife," said Selmer. "They were married in 1930. They lived together only a few months, and so far as I know they were never divorced."

"They were living together again, and he trusted her with a key to the safe-deposit box," said the First Lady.

"I'm sure he didn't," said Selmer. "She was in his house all day every day and had plenty of time to search. She knew about the box because he had rented it in her name, so she had to go to the bank to open it. I imagine he waited outside, and when she came out of the vault I bet you he searched her to make sure she hadn't put anything in her purse or her pockets."

"She had money," grunted Basrak. "Since I've known her, she always had the money to buy anything she wanted."

"How long were you her supplier?" asked Kennelly.

Basrak shrugged. "Six months, about."

"Okay," said Kennelly. He spoke to Selmer. "You didn't know exactly what hour Duroc would die. In fact, you didn't know for sure she'd manage to kill him that particular day. You'd told Angela not to phone you from the White House, 'cause the White House operator might remember Duroc's secretary had called Dan Selmer immediately after Duroc's death—and somebody would have found *that* interesting. You figured on meeting Angela when she came out. Then you'd know. Then you could rush to Duroc's house and confront Toni. You figured you'd make a deal with her. She'd go somewhere with you that night, and in the morning she'd open the box. You'd make some kind of split with her, giving her a few thousand for her trouble— which she would accept because you have a variety of means to persuade her. Then—"

"On the whole, you've got it figured out, Lieutenant," said Selmer unhappily.

"But you had a big surprise coming," Kennelly went on. "Toni found out before you did that Duroc was dead. I don't know if somebody was takin' care of her or she heard it on the radio. The radio, I figure. She grabbed the key and a few clothes and scrammed. You guys are amateurs."

"Then you set to work to track her down," said Mrs. Roosevelt. "And— Well, it seems you knew she was addicted to dope. That made it possible for you to find her supplier and— What is the term, Lieutenant Kennelly?"

" 'Finger her,' " said Kennelly.

Mrs. Roosevelt nodded. "You 'fingered' the unfortunate young woman. How did you know she was addicted?"

"If you'd seen her, you'd have known," said Samuel Paxton. "Dilated pupils. Unnaturally thin. Pallid. Nervous."

"I believe we are very close to having confessions here," said Mrs. Roosevelt.

"We'll get them at headquarters," said Kennelly.

"So . . ." said Mrs. Roosevelt. She began to assemble her papers in a neat pile. "My husband invites me to distance myself from problems of this nature, but—"

"But we couldn't have figured it out if you hadn't helped," said Kennelly.

She smiled. "That is an exaggeration, Lieutenant Kennelly," she said. "But a very gracious one, and I appreciate it. If ever again I can be of some small help, please let me know."

EPILOGUE

When Angela Murphy's fingerprints were taken at police headquarters, she proved to be a professional criminal. She was wanted for another murder and was suspected in two more. She appeared to be, in fact, a young woman who killed for hire.

On Thursday, May 14, 1936, Angela Murphy was hanged in the enclosed courtyard of the District Jail.

Within five minutes she was followed to the gallows by Daniel Selmer.

Samuel Paxton and Ernest McSweeney were sentenced to life imprisonment. Nine weeks later, Paxton died of a heart attack in his cell in the Atlanta Penitentiary. Ernest McSweeney died in prison in 1954.

Bobby Basrak served a year on his conviction for dope dealing, plus four months for carrying a concealed weapon. He was drafted into the armed services in 1942. As a convicted felon, he might have claimed exemption, but he accepted conscription, rose to the rank of staff sergeant, and was killed in action in Italy in 1943.

Terry Rolland was indicted for falsifying accounts and accepting bribes. Her lawyer, John Evans, fell in love with the freckled redhead and struggled to arrange for her to suffer no harsher punishment than a term of probation. He was successful. He married her. After her term of probation ended, they moved to Cincinnati, his home town, and lived there until his death in 1978, hers in 1985. He joined, successively, America First, then the John Birch Society, both of which were useful to success in the practice of law in Cincinnati, and became prosperous, then wealthy. She became a sponsor of a chair in the Cincinnati Symphony and a patroness of the Cincinnati Art Museum. Thérèse Evans, with her faint but amusing southern accent, was a leader of Cincinnati society—keeping it, of course, a deep secret that she had once worked not just for the New Deal but in the Roosevelt White House itself.

After Terry's mother died, her father, Horace Rolland, came to live with his daughter and son-in-law. She bestowed on him the honorific "Colonel," and he was so known in Cincinnati until he died in 1954—Colonel Rolland, ostensibly a Kentucky colonel, though he had never been in Kentucky in his life until he developed the habit of crossing the Ohio River to visit the bawdy houses in Covington. One of those evenings he met the chairman of the Hamilton County Republican Party, which resulted in his being appointed to a vacancy in the office of county recorder, to which office he was subsequently elected twice.

Congressman Devol resigned. Captain Sykes resigned his commission.

Antonia Mathilde Boudreau, the mother of Antonia Caroline Long, lived in Florida until 1976. In 1938 she married Melvin Eberhard, a retiree thirty years her senior. He died in 1951, and she inherited his pleasant beachfront house in Boca Raton.

Stan Szczygiel retired in 1939 and moved to Florida as he had planned. He invested in real estate and became a millionaire. He died in 1961, survived by his wife, Wilma.

Lieutenant Edward Kennelly continued to serve with the District police, rising to the rank of captain. He would work with the First Lady on other mysteries.

Nineteen thirty-six was a busy year for Mrs. Roosevelt. It was also, on the whole, a happy year. But before November and triumphant reelection she would have to give her attention to the strange case of the murder in the White House rose garden.